CHAPTER

ONE

"You only get one wish," said Margot.

I stared at the ten rapidly melting candles on top of my birthday cake. "But I can't choose," I said. A bead of sweat ran down my forehead, partly from the heat of the flames, and partly from the pressure. It felt like everyone in the café was staring at me.

My brother, Fabien, put down his knitting and swiped a finger along the icing. "It's Luna's birthday," he muttered, through a mouthful of stolen buttercream. "If she can't make more than one wish today, then when can she?"

"Exactly," I said.

Margot sighed. "OK, just do it before I turn ninety."

I squeezed my eyes tight and thought about the two things I wanted more than anything else in the world: for Mum to let me have a pet, and for Dad to smile again.

Smoke twirled into my nose as I made my wishes, and I opened my eyes. Mum leaned over the cake and sliced it into four even pieces. A baby on the next table clapped at me, and then got distracted by something over my shoulder. I turned and glanced out of the donkey sanctuary's window at the paddock opposite. Ten donkeys plodded across the grass, their ears pricked to the wind.

"Can I go back outside?" I asked.

"All right, but stay where I can see you," said Mum.

"I'm coming too," said Margot.

"And me!" said Fabien.

We ran back into the hot July afternoon. Most of the donkeys were standing in the middle of the field, their manes billowing in the breeze. I held out my hand and called to them. A grey one lumbered over and nuzzled my cardigan. I took out a packet of mints and fed him one. The donkey nuzzled me again, and then three more came over.

I laughed and stroked their faces. Soon we were surrounded by noses and ears and tongues. I tipped mint after mint on to my hand, and the donkeys gobbled them up gently.

Meow.

Purr, purr, purr.

I looked across the paddock, trying to spot the animal that had made the very un-donkey-like noise. A small ginger cat pranced across the grass and wrapped its tail around the leg of a donkey near the back of the field. The donkey bent its head, looked at the cat and licked a long line right down its back.

The cat rubbed its cheeks against the donkey's legs, and the bell on its pink collar jingled. I gasped as the donkey licked it again, but all the other rescuees ignored it, as if this sort of thing happened all the time.

"You don't think he's going to eat the cat, do you?" I asked Margot, pointing at the donkey.

"Don't be stupid, Luna," she replied, stuffing her hands in her pockets. "They're obviously friends."

"Oh, good," I replied. I'd never met any real donkeys before, but Granny had. Every Sunday, she used to come over for tea and tell us stories. My favourite was about a donkey called Cecil. He'd been her pet when she was little, and Granny had kept a photograph of him on her bedside table. He was cream with black eyes, just like this donkey. She said he was the fastest donkey she'd ever met, and that she used to ride him to school.

I missed Granny's stories. Everything changed when she died. Dad barely spoke any more.

Instead he just spent all day asleep or watching old *Countdown* episodes. He was even missing my birthday treat.

The cat padded towards us, and slipped through the fence into the courtyard we were standing in. Fabien scooped it up, and ran back towards the café with it.

"Look, Mum, I've found a cat!" he yelled, brandishing the purring animal at her through the window.

The donkey plodded over to me, looking sad to have lost his friend. I clicked my tongue and smiled at him. The donkey stared at me with his chocolate-button eyes, pulled back his lips and smiled too.

"Is he…?" I began.

"Copying you!" said Margot.

She was right. The donkey was definitely grinning back at me.

"Wow," I whispered.

"Amazing!" said Margot.

The donkey came right over to me. I stretched out my arm and patted his neck. The donkey's fur was soft and warm like a blanket. I tickled his ears, which were far bigger than my hand, and his breath warmed my face. A yellow collar hung loosely around his neck.

Little Cocoa, 2 years old.

"Little Cocoa," I read aloud. "Is that your name?"

The donkey nuzzled into me, brushing his face against mine. Yes, Little Cocoa it was.

I stroked his nose and Little Cocoa smiled at me again. There was a piece of hay stuck between his wonky teeth, as though he'd been flossing with it. I wondered why he was at the sanctuary. Surely nobody could have given him away?

"Let's adopt him," I said.

Margot laughed. "We live in a flat."

"He could sleep in the bandstand in the park, or we could buy a stable," I said.

"In the middle of London?" asked Margot.

"We could move," I suggested.

"The donkey isn't even for sale," said Margot. "The sanctuary rescues them, and then they live here forever."

"Oh," I replied glumly. "I bet a donkey would make a great pet. They make me think of Granny."

"Me too," smiled Margot, and she draped her arm over my shoulder.

I fed Little Cocoa a mint, and heard a door open in the distance.

"Margot, Luna, time to go," called Mum, from over by the café.

"Five more minutes," I pleaded.

Mum hurried over to us, looking flustered. "Fabien brought a cat into the café, and it's just eaten a lady's scone. It's time we went," she muttered.

I kissed Little Cocoa on the nose, and traipsed after Mum. It had been the best birthday trip ever, because now I knew exactly what pet I wanted. And it wasn't a cat, or a dog, or a hamster. It was a donkey.

It was dinner time when we arrived back at our flat. I pushed open the door and saw a piece of paper on the mat. Somebody must have pushed it under the door. Fabien picked it up.

"What does 'eviction' mean?" he asked.

"Let's see," said Margot, snatching the letter away. She scanned her eyes across it and all the colour drained from her usually bright face. "Oh, my God. They're chucking us out!"

Mum read the letter over Margot's shoulder,

and went all pale.

I turned to Margot, panicked. "Who's chucking us out?" I asked.

"The landlord," she squeaked.

"He can't do that! We live here," I said.

"It says we haven't paid the rent for three months," said Margot.

It was three months ago that Dad had stopped going to work. He'd always hated his job at the prison, and when Granny died he just stopped going. Mum had tried to get more hours at the supermarket, but her manager said there weren't any. She'd told us not to worry, and that everything would be OK. I guessed that was a lie.

Dad poked his head out of the bedroom, and rubbed his eyes. There were dark circles beneath them like storm clouds. He was still in yesterday's pyjamas, even though it was late. A line of biscuit crumbs covered his hairy top lip.

"What's all the commotion about?" he asked.

Margot showed him the letter, and Dad wobbled into a heap in the doorway.

"It'll be all right," I said, draping my arm around him, although I wasn't sure it would.

Fabien fetched his piggy bank and emptied

the contents into Dad's lap. "You can have my savings. There's forty pounds and sixteen pence."

"We need a bit more than that," croaked Mum.

I swallowed, hard. We were going to be homeless.

CHAPTER

TWO

"We need a plan," I said as I poured myself a bowl of economy chocolate rice pops the next morning.

Margot put down her latest copy of *Aeroplanes Monthly* magazine. "What we need is money."

"Do you think the local shop will give me a paper round?" I asked.

"No, and we need more money than that anyway," she said.

I crunched my cereal miserably. "What if I chain myself to the electricity meter? They can't make us leave then."

"You might get fried," said Margot.

Fabien poked his head around the door. "What's getting fried? Is it bacon?"

"No, Luna's head," replied Margot.

"Yuck," he said, and then skated across the lino in his worn-out socks. "I've found us somewhere to live."

"Where?" I asked.

He threw a newspaper across the table at me. It was the free one that got delivered every week. I knew Fabien was good at papier mâché, but even *he* couldn't make a house out of this.

"Read page five," he said.

I found the page and read the article aloud.

Bonkers businessman gives away island

Eric Harding, founder of Rhino Technologies, is giving away his Scottish island.

The lonely billionaire has gifted dozens of things over the past ten years, including a helicopter to a man from Norway, a Hollywood sushi restaurant to a monk from Tibet, and a herd of Highland cattle to St John's School in Hythe. He also arranged for pensioner Betty Eccles to fulfil her lifetime dream of abseiling down Big Ben naked.

When asked to comment on his latest giveaway, Mr Harding said, "My daughter used to love Rook's Island, but I haven't visited it since I lost her. I hope somebody will fall in love with it, just like my Cassy did, and bring joy to the island again."

This is one of Mr Harding's biggest and most eccentric giveaways, topped only by the donation of his Borneo estate to two university students. When last heard of, the pair had put their accountancy studies on hold to raise orangutans in the jungle. It's believed they have since branched out into gorilla breeding.

As part of the competition's terms and conditions, the island can never be sold by the winner. Anyone who enters should therefore be prepared to live in the middle of the ocean for the rest of their natural life.

To enter the competition, simply email assistant@ ericharding.com or write to PO Box 828, London SW19, stating why you want to win.

About the closing date, Mr Harding simply said, "How long is a strand of spaghetti?"

Below the newspaper article was a colour photo of the island, with a big, wonky house and a herd of goats. It looked beautiful, the sun melting into the sea, and the waves all shimmery shiny.

"Look!" I said, shoving the article under Margot's nose.

She laughed. "Nobody actually wins these things, you two."

"Someone must!" said Fabien.

"He's right," I replied. "Wouldn't it be amazing to live on our very own island?"

Margot shook her head. "No, I think the whole thing sounds awful. We'd have to move away from our friends. And who wants to live in the middle of the sea?"

"I do," I replied.

"Me too," said Fabien. "There are animals!"

The whole thing sounded amazing. We'd have our own beach, and could go swimming in the sea every morning. Even better, the island looked big enough to have a hundred pets. I could probably get a whole drove of donkeys and Mum wouldn't even notice.

My heart fluttered with excitement. Dad would be so happy if we won the island. It would be like being on a permanent holiday. There was no way he could still be sad then.

I grabbed a sheet of paper, and began to write a letter to Mr Harding in my neatest handwriting. Maybe Margot was right and nobody did win these things, but it was worth a try.

Dear Mr Harding,

I read in the newspaper that you're giving away your island. That's really kind of you. I bet you're the most generous person in the whole world – much more generous than the Queen, or Angelina Jolie, or Mr Phoon from the takeaway (although he does give us free chips on a Wednesday, which is very nice of him)...

I explained all about Dad losing his job, and

how we were being evicted, and how I'd finally be able to get my own pet if we won the island. It was the longest letter I'd ever written. My skin got goosebumpy with excitement as I folded it up, and tucked it neatly into an envelope.

"Now I just need to post it," I said.

Fabien pranced over to me with something blue and fluffy in his arms.

"You can send him these as a present," he said.

"What are they?" I asked.

"Knitted dolphin slippers, of course," said Fabien.

I nudged the knitted monstrosities. The "slippers" were grey with blue flecks. The toes were knitted into a pointed nose, and there were strange sticky-out bits, which I assumed were the flippers. On the top, a pair of googly eyes jiggled about.

"I'm not sure if he'll need new slippers," I replied carefully.

Fabien's face dropped. "Don't you like them?"

"Of course I do!" I said quickly, trying to undo the hurt look on his face. "They're very … different."

He beamed. "Limited edition."

"Thank goodness," whispered Margot.

Fabien squeezed the slippers into a Jiffy bag, and sealed my letter inside. I hoped they would magically un-knit themselves in the post.

CHAPTER

THREE

The phone rang.

Everyone ignored it.

The phone rang some more.

Mum packed our gravy granules into a moving box, and then started on the spice rack. We were going to be homeless in two days, and all the council had found us was a room in a bed and breakfast. I'd looked it up on Google Maps, and zoomed into the image of its smeary door. There was a sign on it that said NO PETS ALLOWED in really big, angry letters. This was a disaster. There was probably more chance of me turning *into* an animal than keeping one there.

"Could somebody please answer the phone?" asked Mum.

I followed the ringing sound to the bedroom I shared with Margot. The door was closed, and there was a sign taped to it that said DO NOT DISTURB – FLIGHT IN PROGRESS. I pressed my ear to the door and the ringing got louder.

"Margot, what are you doing?" I asked, barging in.

My sister was perched on her bed, staring at Dad's laptop with a joystick in her hands. I craned my neck around the screen and saw a virtual aeroplane bank around a volcano. Underneath Margot's elbow was a book called *How to Fly a Boeing 747: Volume 9.*

"I'm flying to Indonesia," she said. "Just about to start my descent."

"Where's the phone?"

"There isn't one," said Margot. "We use radios up here."

"I mean the *real* phone," I said. "Can't you hear it ringing?"

"Oh, now that you mention it…" she replied, and trailed off as her plane flew through a cloud.

I found the phone inside my underwear drawer, although I couldn't remember putting it there. The display flashed EXTERNAL CALL, which seemed kind of obvious. I pressed the green button, and held the phone to my ear. A dial tone buzzed at me. The caller must have hung up just as I answered.

"Oh, well," I said, and tucked the phone back under a sock.

The bedroom door swung open again, and I looked up to see Fabien trot inside with an empty box in his arms. He dropped to his knees beside my bed, and scrabbled around underneath, as if fishing for dust mites. I knelt beside him and peered into the box. It was full of knitting needles and half-finished jumpers.

"Aha!" exclaimed Fabien, and he pulled out a ball of sparkling purple wool. "Knew I'd left it here."

I hugged my knees to my chest. There wasn't enough room in the bed and breakfast for Fabien's knitting, or Margot's flying books, or my stuffed animals. We were going to have to leave everything behind. Poor Fabien. He probably thought it was going to be a big adventure.

The phone rang again, and my drawer started to vibrate. I pulled it open and grabbed the phone. It was probably just a salesman. Maybe I could put on a grown-up voice and ask for a job. I could sell windows, and help with the rent on a new flat.

I pressed the phone to my ear, and this time it didn't buzz at me. "Hello?" I said.

"Hello, is this the Butterworth residence?" asked a voice. It belonged to an old-sounding man.

"Yes, this is Luna Butterworth speaking," I said, making each word sound loud and proper. "Are you selling conservatories?"

"Er, no," he said.

"Oh. Magazine subscriptions?" I asked.

"Noooo," he said.

"Package holidays to Spain?" I tried.

"I'm calling about a letter I received from you, regarding a little island of mine," said the caller.

My heart thumped so loudly that I was sure the man could hear it down the phone. My mouth turned as dry as one of Mum's pasta bakes, and my knees wobbled into each other. I collapsed on to Margot's duvet, and almost dropped the phone.

Margot paused her flight and turned to me. "Who is it?" she asked.

I put the phone on loudspeaker.

"Let me introduce myself," said the man. "My name is Mr Harding."

Margot choked. "Did he say Mr Harding?"

The caller chuckled. "Yes, I did. To whom am I speaking now?"

"Margot..." said Margot, her eyes full of suspicion.

"And me!" yelled Fabien, before adding, "Who's Mr Harding?"

"The man with the island," I sputtered.

Fabien squealed and bounced up like an excited puppy. "Mr Billionaire!"

"Yes, I'm Mr Billionaire," the voice chuckled. "My assistant only handed me your letter today. I wasn't sure whether I'd still be able to reach you on this number."

"You ... you read my letter?" I asked.

"Yes, of course. It was a very good letter, although I was sad to hear about your current predicament with your landlord," he said.

This couldn't be real. It had to be a joke, somebody from school playing tricks on us. Maybe it was Great-Uncle Stan with a voice distorter. It couldn't really be Mr Billionaire, could it?

"I must say," he continued, "your letter reminded me very much of my daughter, Cassy, especially the part about you liking donkeys. She was a great animal lover. Loved anything with a paw or hoof. Scales too, for that matter."

"It did?" I squeaked. "You really liked my letter?"

Fabien leaned over the phone. "Did you like the slippers I knitted you?"

"Oh, yes, I thought they were smashing. They'll

be just perfect for my holiday mansion in Sweden. Gets very cold there in winter," he said. "It's been years since anybody's given me such a thoughtful present. I've been smiling down at them ever since. Very stylish and practical."

I glanced at Fabien and his ears glowed with bashfulness. Now I knew this had to be a joke. Nobody in their right mind would think Fabien's slippers were stylish, let alone a billionaire. Then again, Mr Billionaire didn't sound much like he *was* in his right mind.

"Are your parents available? I'd very much like to speak with them," continued Mr Billionaire.

Margot shook her head and mimed strangling me. "They're out," she said.

"Ah, that's a shame," said Mr Billionaire. "Perhaps I should call back later."

"No!" I exclaimed. "They're not out, they're—"

"Away. On holiday. In China," interrupted Margot.

The bedroom door creaked open and Mum poked her head inside. "Who's in China?"

"You are," said Fabien.

"Am I?"

Margot leapt up and pushed her back out

through the door. "Mum, can you help me with my homework in the kitchen?"

"Who's on the phone?" she asked suspiciously.

Mr Billionaire's voice boomed out through the speaker. "My name is Mr Harding. Is that Mrs Butterworth?"

"Yes!" I yelled, and threw the phone at Mum.

Mum took the phone off speaker and pressed it to her ear. I watched her face turn white as she listened to Mr Billionaire, and then she made a strange sort of squeaking sound. Margot grabbed at the phone frantically, but Mum swatted her away and staggered out into the hallway.

I jumped up and raced after her, but Mum slammed her bedroom door in my face. There was a clicking sound, like she'd turned the lock. I pressed down on the door handle, but it wouldn't budge. She'd shut herself and Dad inside.

"Do you think it's really him?" I asked Margot.

"I don't know," she replied, voice shaky.

"Do you think we've won?" I asked.

"I don't know," she replied again.

"I've never won anything before, apart from that window squeegee in the Christmas raffle," I said.

We sat outside the door for more than an hour. My fingers went numb from crossing them so tightly. Margot tapped her feet nervously until a hole appeared in her socks, and Fabien bounced up and down as if on an invisible trampoline. The seconds felt like minutes, and the minutes like eternity.

Finally the bedroom door opened, and we rushed inside. Mum and Dad were sitting at the end of the bed, looking shaken. A map was stretched across the floor.

"Was it really him?" I asked. "Have we won the island?"

Mum nodded without a word.

"We've won!" I sputtered. I took Fabien's hand and twirled around in circles with him. "We've won, we've won, we've won!"

"Luna," whispered Dad, but I could barely hear him.

"We've won an island!"

"Luna," said Dad again.

"A real island of our very own!"

"LUNA!" shouted Dad, and I stopped jumping. It was the loudest he'd spoken in months. "Luna, we're not moving there."

My excitement vanished. "What do you mean?"

"We're not moving there," said Dad.

"Why not?" I asked.

"It's just not sensible," said Mum. "Mr Harding will have to give the island to somebody else."

"But we're going to be homeless!" I said. "At least we'll have a house to stay in on the island."

Margot glanced out of the window. "I don't want to leave London. We're directly under the New York flight path. I can plane-spot without having to leave my bedroom."

"I'm sure they have planes in Scotland," I said.

"What about school, and my friends?" she asked.

"They could visit," I said. "And Dad could home-school us."

"You mean there'd be no more school? Like, ever?" asked Margot.

"No, and Mum would have loads of space for her stretchy thing," I said.

Mum's eyes lit up. "I could run my own yoga retreats."

"See, it's brilliant!" I said, and then turned to Dad. "Granny would have thought so too. She loved Scotland."

Dad stared at the photo of Granny on the bedside table, and his face turned all sad and tired. I missed Dad's smile. If he just gave the island a chance, I was sure he'd find it again.

"I could grow my own wool!" shouted Fabien, leaping into the air as if struck by lightning.

"You don't grow wool," sighed Margot. "And I'm not moving to the island, even if it does mean no more school. Absolutely no way."

I folded my arms. "We'll see about that."

CHAPTER

FOUR

"I can't believe I agreed to this," said Dad as our taxi sped along the endless Scottish countryside.

"This is the worst idea ever," said Margot. "*And the plane journey here was too short.*"

Rain sloshed down the windscreen, and sheep huddled on the rolling hills. I tapped my feet with excitement, and kept my eyes on the road ahead. Soon I was going to see our island. It was the most brilliant day of my entire life.

"Will I have to wear a kilt?" asked Fabien.

"Of course not," replied Margot.

"Will I get a bagpipe?" he asked.

"I hope not," she said.

"What about my own dinghy?"

"Maybe on Thursdays," said Margot.

We turned off the main road as she said this, and I leaned forward. Outside the window was a row of wonky houses, with stone chimneys, and red bunting strung between the roofs. I opened the window and took a deep breath. The air smelled of salt and fish.

"Looks like we're here," said Mum as we crested a hill.

The land dropped away and the sea appeared. It stretched all the way to the grey horizon. Rusty fishing boats lined the harbour, and men hauled crates off them. Gulls circled the catch with begging beaks, as ice sloshed everywhere.

I looked into the distance, and my heart thudded. Sandwiched in between the sea and sky was an island. It was so far away, I could barely see it. If I squinted, it looked a bit like an inky smudge beneath the sun.

"Is that it?" I asked.

"I think so," replied Mum. "Mr Harding said it's visible from land."

The car stopped, and I flung off my seatbelt and jumped out. An escaped crab dashed past my foot, claws clicking. A gust of wind ruffled my top, and filled my lungs with salty air. We definitely weren't in London any more.

Fabien danced around me. "This is brilliant! It's just like being at the seaside."

"We *are* at the seaside," said Margot.

"Isn't it great?" I asked.

She shot daggers at me. "I'm in hell."

"Come on, let's go!" I said.

"Hold your horses," replied Mum. "Mr Harding said we have to find a man called Doug. He's the person who rents out the boats."

"Try the pub," said our taxi driver.

I picked up my suitcase and started to walk. Beyond the harbour was a row of stone buildings, with glass shopfronts. The last one had a wooden sign above it that said *The Wig and Pen*. The smell of old beer and pork scratchings wafted out of it.

"That must be it," I said, crossing the road.

There was a menu in the window, which seemed to consist entirely of different variations of battered fish. I pushed open the door, but instead of being greeted by the sight of a normal pub, I found a room lined with stacks of shelves. Each one was piled with things like bread, toilet rolls and tinned tomatoes. In the middle of the room were a dozen empty tables, their surfaces sticky with glass marks, and at the far end was a bar. A little post office was tagged on to the end of it.

"Hello there," called a woman from behind the till. "I'm Heidi. Can I get you a drink, or a loaf of bread?"

"You're a pub *and* a shop?" asked Margot.

"Yes, but we don't sell Cheddar," shuddered Heidi.

"Of course not..." replied Margot. "Do you

have Wi-Fi?"

"We have a computer in the corner," she said, pointing to a clumpy old desktop. There was a sign on it that read *50p for three hours.*

"Is that it?" asked Margot.

Heidi smiled. "You're not from round here, are you?"

"We're from London!" said Fabien. "We've come to see our island."

Heidi's eyes grew wide. "*You're* the family who won Rook's Island!" she exclaimed.

"Yes!" I said, unable to contain my excitement.

"Goodness! Sit down and I'll fetch you some tea. You must be exhausted after such a long journey," she said.

"Thank you, but we need to find somebody called Doug. Apparently, he can rent us a boat so we can reach the island before nightfall," said Mum.

"Doug's my brother, but he's not been in today," replied Heidi.

"Oh…" I said, deflating like a popped balloon.

"He's probably at the boat shack. I'll ask my son, Kai, to take you there," she replied.

Heidi called up the stairs behind her, and a

few moments later a boy came down them. He looked about my age, with dark, messy hair, and what appeared to be sawdust on his knees.

"Follow me," huffed Kai.

We had to jog to keep up with him as he led us around the harbour. Scraps of sawdust flaked from his jeans, and I wondered what he'd been doing.

"Do you have a pet?" I asked him, panting.

"I rescue rabbits," he said, not turning to me.

"Really? From where?" I asked.

Kai continued to march on without looking at me. "From all over the place. I rehome them."

"Like an animal shelter?" I asked.

"Suppose so," he replied.

I thought about Kai's rabbit shelter, and an idea struck me. I could open my very own donkey sanctuary, just like the one I'd visited on my birthday, and Kai could tell me all about how to do it. After all, rescuing rabbits couldn't be all that different to rescuing donkeys. Meeting him was clearly a sign.

Before I could ask him any more questions, Kai came to a stop outside a shack near the water. It was surrounded by rickety boats, and I listened to them creak as Kai knocked on the door. The whole building wobbled as if it was about to topple over. Mum and Dad looked a bit pale.

"All right, Uncle Doug?" asked Kai. "I've bought customers."

Doug poked his head out of the shack and looked us over. He had the same dark, shaggy hair as Kai. A patchy beard covered his chin, and I noticed there was a squashed pea stuck in the wispy bit.

"Customers?" he asked. "Blimey. I haven't had a customer in eight months."

He lumbered outside, and the scent of instant noodles followed him. It wasn't hard to see why he hadn't had any customers. Most of his boats were held together with gaffer tape and wine corks.

"This is *Lady Agatha*, my finest boat," said Doug.

Tied up to the harbour wall was a hunk of metal that swayed in the water. A scribble of faded paint spelled out her name on the side. I touched it, and a scab of rust flaked on to my fingertips.

Margot folded her arms. "That's not a boat – it's a tuna tin."

"Do you have any others?" asked Mum.

"None so buoyant," replied Doug.

"I want to drive it!" said Fabien, and he jumped on to the deck, startling a seagull that was perched on the steering wheel.

I whispered to Kai, "Is it safe?"

"Probably. It's been a while since she last sank," he replied, and with that he turned and left us.

"What do you mean 'sank'?" I called after him, but he didn't answer.

I took a deep breath, climbed down into the boat and grabbed a lifejacket. My trainers squeaked on the deck, and I noticed there was a hole in the boat, plugged with chewing gum. The whole deck tilted to one side.

There was a key in the ignition, ready for us to turn. I stood at the wheel and looked at the horizon, at our island. It was so close I could probably swim there, although it would take a while.

"Look, I'm a fish!" said Fabien, who had wrapped a net around his legs.

"You look more like a mermaid," I said, trying to pull him free. "Hold still, would you?"

"But I like it," he said.

Margot shimmied on board, and marched towards us with her hands on her hips. Mum was thumbing through a health and safety manual that Doug had given her, and Dad was staring out to sea with a worried look on his face.

"Stop messing around, you two — it's dangerous," said Margot.

"I'm trying to help him!" I protested.

"I don't need help," said Fabien.

He kicked his legs, and more of the net snaked around him.

Margot yanked Fabien free in one movement. "This is going to be an absolute disaster."

I listened to Doug explain how the boat worked to Mum, and then finally we set off. We went slowly at first as she got used to the controls, and then faster and faster. The sea ahead was clear, like an empty road. Water sprayed my face in an icy mist, and the wind blew my ponytail out.

The harbour shrank behind us. With every wave we crested, the island grew bigger and bigger. The trees became greener, and the beach more golden. My heart beat faster.

Soon the island was all I could see.

CHAPTER

FIVE

My trainers sank into the sand.

"We're here!" I yelled. "We're really here!"

"Wait for us," said Mum as she struggled to untie her three lifejackets. Dad didn't move.

I ran across the beach, which unfolded like a golden ribbon. It was covered with shells and pebbles and washed-up seaweed. The sand spilled into my socks. Small red birds swooped across the sky and butterflies fluttered through the pine trees ahead.

"Look, Luna!" said Fabien.

He was crouched beside a set of animal tracks. I squinted through the fading light, and knelt down to examine them. The tracks wove across the beach in pairs. They had two toes, like a deer's hoof.

"Is it a sheep?" asked Fabien.

I tried to think of what a sheep's foot looked like, but couldn't. One thing was certain, these prints didn't belong to a donkey.

"I'm not sure," I said. "It's definitely some kind of animal though."

"Cool!" replied Fabien.

Margot knelt beside us, and picked up a handful of sand. She let it trickle through her fingers, catching the delicate shells. They reminded me of the soap in Granny's bathroom, which was always shaped like clams.

"This might make a good runway," said Margot. "I've always wanted to try a beach take-off."

"That's silly," said Fabien.

"You'd sink," I said.

Margot tutted at us. "You don't know anything about planes."

I grabbed my suitcase and tugged it across the beach. In front of us was a wall of trees, thick and tall. I craned my neck to the canopy, but couldn't see the top.

"I'm going to build my own beach hut," said Fabien, skidding over to me. "A big blue one with a green roof."

"Never mind a beach hut – just think of the stables I could have!" I said.

"What about the house?" asked Margot.

"There's already a house here. We don't need to build one of those," I said.

"I *know* that," replied Margot. "But where is it?"

Mum clambered off the boat, and pulled Dad behind her. "Does anyone have the map Mr

Harding sent?"

"No, you had it last. How are we going to find the house without the map? We can't stay out here – we'll be eaten by wolves," said Margot.

"Well, I know it's somewhere in the middle of the island," replied Mum, gesturing vaguely with her hand.

"I'll use my compass," said Fabien, and he got out a little plastic one.

"Where did you get that?" asked Margot.

"Last year's Christmas cracker," he replied. "But it really works!"

We followed Fabien and his compass through the trees, and the sandy floor changed to cracked mud under my feet. Branches scratched my arms, and leaves dangled down on my head. It was cold in their shade, and scarily dark.

I grabbed hold of the tree trunks, and pulled myself up the hill. It was steep, and my trainers slipped on the fallen leaves. A set of animal tracks wove across our path – the same ones that were on the beach.

"These trees will have to go," grumbled Dad, tripping over a root. A bird swooped down on him, as if in protest.

"No, we have to keep them!" said Fabien. "I can sledge around them when it snows, like an obstacle course."

"Trees are very good for balancing your zen," added Mum.

"I think something's been eating them," said Margot, and she pointed to a gnawed trunk.

I sucked in a sharp breath. "Donkeys eat tree bark."

Maybe there were already donkeys on the island, wild ones with nobody to care for them. I could build them a home and look after them. They could be the first residents of my sanctuary.

The trees thinned, and we emerged on to a field. Knee-high grass tickled my feet, and a bee buzzed past my ear. I saw the outline of a house in the distance. It was huge, almost the size of a mansion. Vines climbed up the brickwork, twisted around the windows and swallowed the front door. It must have been empty for ages.

I heard something rustle in the grass ahead, and a small tail swished through the green blades. My breath caught. Was it a donkey foal?

"Goat!" yelled Fabien as he shoved past me.

A melon-sized head poked out from the grass,

with square eyes and floppy ears. A pair of horns curved down like a funny hat. My heart sank; it definitely wasn't a donkey.

Maaaaa, the goat yelled. *Maaaaa.*

Margot shook her head. "That's all we need, a bunch of goats eating everything."

"Look at its coat!" said Fabien. "It's *so woolly*!"

Through the grass, I saw the goat was covered in tight, muddy ringlets. The sight of them made Fabien's face glow like a Christmas tree. It was obvious that he was dreaming of scarves and bobble hats.

Margot shuddered. "I don't like its horns."

"It's perfect," said Fabien dreamily.

He inched closer, arms outstretched, but the goat bounded off.

"Wait, come back!" he called, and sped after it.

Margot rugby-tackled him. "Leave it. It's going to be dark soon."

"But I might never see it again," whimpered Fabien.

"There'll be plenty of time for sheep-shearing later," said Margot.

"Goat-shearing," Fabien corrected her scornfully.

"Come on," I said, pulling Fabien by the sleeve.

We carried on towards the house, and a shiver ran down my spine. Up close, I saw the windows were black with dust, and one of them was cracked. Tangled rose bushes guarded the front of the house, and the doorstep was littered with fallen roof tiles. A crow flexed its wings on the chimney and cawed.

I yanked on the vines covering the door, but they clung tight. A spider crept across them, and a moth landed on my hand. I shuddered and shook it off.

Margot helped me tug the vines loose to uncover the door handle. I took the key from Mum and wriggled it in the lock. It clicked once, and the door creaked open.

Dust swirled up as I shoved my way inside. I covered my mouth as I choked on the stale air. The hallway was dark and narrow. Mum found the light switch and a bulb flickered on.

"It's filthy!" exclaimed Mum.

"It's a death trap!" corrected Margot.

"It's not that bad," I said.

Fabien puffed on his inhaler. "Do you think I can make dust angels?"

"Don't you dare," said Mum.

Dad looked even more miserable than he had in London. I bit my lip, and hoped he'd like the rest of the house better. If winning the island didn't cheer up Dad then nothing would.

I tried not to think about it, and headed towards the stairs. "I'm going to pick my bedroom."

"Oh no you're not," said Margot. "I should get first pick, seeing as you dragged me here."

"I should get the biggest room because I'm the youngest," announced Fabien.

The three of us locked eyes, and then bolted up the stairs in an explosion of dust. I elbowed Margot out of the way, but Fabien pirouetted around me and army-rolled into the first room. It was huge, with a grand four-poster bed in the middle. I wondered whether to fight him for it, but Margot's footsteps were coming up quickly behind me, so I decided to cut my losses and make a dash for the next one.

The door creaked open on its old hinges, and I dived through it. The room was even bigger than the one Fabien had chosen, with a bay window that overlooked the clearing and the forest. Across the treetops, I could see all the way to the beach, and beyond the water the soft lights of the mainland. It was the perfect lookout for spotting smugglers, or donkey thieves.

"This bedroom is mi—" I began but, before I could finish, a high-pitched scream filled the house.

My tummy jolted, and I raced out of my bedroom. The noise had come from downstairs. A lump rose in my throat. Had something happened to Dad? Whatever it was, it must have been really bad to make Mum scream like that.

I hurried downstairs with Margot and Fabien, and we found our parents huddled against the wall at the far end of the corridor. As far as I could see, they still had both their arms and legs. I wondered what had happened.

"What's going on?" called Margot.

"Bats," said Mum. "In the kitchen. Thousands of them!"

I peered inside the room at the end of the corridor. It was a large kitchen, with big wooden worktops and a range cooker. I looked at the floor and gasped. The tiles were covered in piles of brown droppings, and a putrid smell wafted up from them.

Fabien pointed to the ceiling, and I looked up. Dozens of bats hung upside down from the swirly plaster, their wings wrapped neatly around them. It was like Mr Billionaire had forgotten to take down the Halloween decorations.

"Does this mean I can keep goats in the kitchen?" asked Fabien.

"Absolutely not!" said Mum.

I turned to Margot, half expecting her to look green with horror. Instead, her eyes were wide and her mouth was open in fascination.

"I've always wanted to study the aerodynamics of bats," she said.

Dad shook his head. "This place is cursed."

"What on earth am I going to say to my yoga-retreat guests?" asked Mum.

"We'll get rid of them," I replied. "I mean the bats, not the yoga people."

Fabien stood up on his tiptoes and whispered to me, "But how, Luna?"

I stared at the sleeping ceiling, and realised I had no idea.

CHAPTER

SIX

I woke up with my face next to a mop. Dust drifted around me, and a spider scurried past and disappeared through a crack in the floorboards. I blinked and tried to remember where I was. This wasn't my bedroom.

There was a blanket over my shoulders. It smelled strange, like damp clothes. I pulled it off and sat up. Margot and Fabien were squished on to a sofa in the corner. Fabien's little legs dangled off the end like string. Cobwebs mummified Margot's hair.

I tried to remember how I'd ended up asleep on the floor. We'd been exploring the house and I remembered that, when it got dark, we'd stopped to light a fire in the living room. The embers were still a deep red. We must have fallen asleep next to it.

Margot ground her teeth, as she always did when waking up. "What time is it?" she asked.

I looked around for a clock. There was one on the coffee table, but its hands were stuck at a quarter to three. I went to check the time on the TV, but then realised there wasn't one. There wasn't much of anything in the living room, apart from the old furniture. Our things from home weren't due to be delivered for another few days yet.

A handful of dead flies lined the window ledge. I brushed them off and opened the curtains. Smoke twisted past the glass, and disappeared into the bright sunshine.

I opened the window and leaned outside. Mum was bending over a barbecue in her pink pyjamas, with a set of tongs in her hand. The smell of smouldering charcoal wafted inside.

"Morning, Luna!" she called. "Come and get some breakfast."

"What is it?" I asked.

"A feast," she replied.

Margot wrinkled her nose. "I hope it's not grilled seaweed."

I ran over to Fabien and shook his feet. "Wake up, we've got an island to explore!"

"Go 'way," he mumbled, eyes squeezed shut.

"But it's morning," I said.

Margot elbowed me. "Let him sleep."

"There's no time for sleep," I said. "Don't you want to find your goats, Fabien?"

Fabien's eyes sprang open. "Goats? Where?"

"Here, on the island," I said.

His forehead furrowed with confusion, and then he leapt off the sofa. "The island! We're on the island!"

"Yes, that's what I'm trying to tell you," I said.

Margot sighed. "Why is everyone so happy about this?"

I grabbed her and Fabien by the arm, and pulled them out to the porch. A convoy of ants shuffled past us, hauling leaves. I jumped over them and landed on the thistle-thick grass. A strong gust of wind blew my hair everywhere.

Something on the barbecue sizzled loudly, and I hovered over it to see what it was. A frazzled lump spat on the grill, and a pot of pale mush bubbled away. My tummy lurched.

"What's that?" I asked Mum.

"Spam with pea soup," she said. "It was all I had in my handbag."

"Who carries Spam and soup in their handbag?" grumbled Margot.

I stood downwind. "Where's Dad?"

"Asleep. He needs his rest at the moment," replied Mum.

I sighed. The island was supposed to make him better, but it hadn't. Dad was still broken, and I had no idea how to fix him.

Fabien tried a spoonful and choked. "I'm not hungry. Can I go and find my goat?"

"All right, but take some Spam just in case," said Mum.

"I'm *not* staying here another day," said Margot.

Fabien ignored her, and sprinted off into the distance. I grabbed Margot's hand and dragged her along after him. Prickly seeds stuck to my T-shirt like Velcro, and a nettle stung my ankle. Our island was a tangle of weeds, colourful flowers and zippy insects. It seemed like the field stretched on for ages, but then suddenly the land tumbled away, and all I could see was the glittering water ahead.

A stitch jabbed my side. Fabien reached the edge of the cliff and skidded to a halt. I stopped beside him, and looked down over the rocky ledge. The height made me feel dizzy.

Jagged grey rocks sloped into the sea, too steep to climb down. Boulders lay at the bottom, as though part of the cliff had crumbled. I wondered how recently. Waves washed over the fallen rocks and seaweed collected at the edges. A seagull bobbed on the water like a rubber duck.

Margot waved her phone in the air.

"What are you doing?" I asked her.

"Trying to call for a taxi," she replied.

"We're on an island…" I told her, slowly.

"A boat taxi," she said. "But I can't find a signal."

"Oh, that's a shame," I replied.

Fabien turned around. "Where do you think the goat is?"

"I'm not sure, but we'll find it," I said.

Margot put her hands on her hips. "I'm going back."

"Won't you help me find my goat?" said Fabien. "Pleeeeease."

Margot stared at him, hard, and then sighed. "*Fine*. But after that I'm going back to wait at the boat until you both realise how ridiculous this whole island thing is."

I smiled at Margot and linked my arm through hers. Hopefully Fabien's goat would stay hidden all day. The longer Margot spent on the island, the more chance there was that she'd fall in love with it, and forget all about London and its flight paths.

We walked alongside the cliff edge, up a hill

and then down again. Our path forced us through the trees, until we emerged on to another beach. Fabien consulted his compass, and told us we were on the northern side of the island. The beach there was a bit smaller than the main one, but beautiful and sun drenched. I wanted to stop and splash in the waves, but Fabien made us march on in search of his goat.

A dozen rock pools seemed to cover the western shore. The water shone grey and green, like jewels. I ran over to the first and peered through its glassy surface. A shoal of silver fish darted away, and a crab scuttled into a nook.

Fabien hopped, skidded and slipped over the pools. "Look, sea snails!" he said, and plucked one off the rock.

Margot shuddered. "Don't touch it – you don't know where it's been."

"Yes, I do," said Fabien. "It's been in the sea."

My stomach rumbled. "Is it edible?"

Fabien tried to lick the snail, but Margot batted it away. "We're in Scotland, not France. Here, I've got some chocolate in my pocket."

She broke the bar into three pieces, and we sat on the edge of the rocks to eat it. I slipped off my shoes and dipped my toes into the water, splashing them to keep the fish at bay. It was icy cold, despite the sun.

"I still haven't found my goat," said Fabien.

"He's probably in the woods," replied Margot.

Fabien scrambled to his feet and skipped towards the trees behind us, singing, "Here, goat, here!"

I tugged my shoes back on, and followed him into the wood. Birds called to each other from their leafy perches. It was as if they wanted to know what we were doing on their island. Perhaps they'd never seen people before.

"Goat fur!" shouted Fabien, and he stooped to examine a piece snagged on a branch.

The tree's trunk had been stripped of bark. I ran my hand over it, and felt teeth marks on the injured wood. A blob of drool stuck to my finger. Fabien's goat had been here, and recently.

"Look, there's more over here," I said, plucking a tuft of fur from another gnawed tree. The branches must have acted like a hairbrush.

"It's a trail!" said Fabien.

We followed the fur like a trail of breadcrumbs. In the distance, a twig snapped and something rustled. I froze, and Margot held out her arm like a barrier. It was only then that I realised how dark and remote our little jungle was.

"That sounded like a footstep," she said.

"Maybe it's Mum?" I replied.

Fabien dropped to his hands and knees. "Shh, you'll scare them."

"Scare who?" whispered Margot. "What are you doing down there?"

"Being a goat," he said.

I looked in the direction that Fabien was facing, and saw six goats halfway up a tree. They were balanced on the branches, their teeth chomping back and forth. The goats weren't just tree eaters: they were acrobats.

Fabien crawled slowly towards them, head bowed. He bleated in his best goat voice, and pretended to eat a leaf. The goats stopped what they were doing, and stared at him. It was as if they weren't sure exactly what he was. They weren't the only ones.

"He could do with a tail," I whispered to Margot.

She sighed. "My family are nuts."

Fabien was only a few metres from the goats now. He lifted his head slightly, and the nearest goat took a step towards him. It was all going surprisingly well, but then suddenly Fabien sprang into the air, and flapped his arms around like a demented pigeon.

"Spider!" he yelled. "Up my sleeve!"

Margot rushed over to Fabien. The spider flew out of his sleeve and scuttled off into the undergrowth. I doubled over with laughter, while the goats jumped off the tree and fled.

"You scared them," said Fabien.

"Me!" I exclaimed.

"Which way did they go?" he asked, but took off without waiting for an answer.

I ran hard to keep up with him. Fabien negotiated the tree roots with all the agility of a mountain goat, while I caught my foot in a rabbit hole and tripped. One of my shoelaces had worked its way loose, and I paused to tie it. As I stooped, something caught my eye through the trees, and my heart thudded.

It was a stable block.

"Wait!" I yelled. "Look at this!"

I abandoned my shoelace, and hurried over to the stables. There were four of them joined together in a row. I opened the first door and stepped inside. Several earwigs fell on my feet, and I shook them off with a groan. Vines crept across the ceiling, and leaves covered the stone floor. The stable was old and run down, but the walls seemed solid. It would be the perfect place to house my rescue donkeys.

There was a blanket in the next one, with something large and bulky hidden underneath. I grabbed a bamboo stick and poked the edge. The blanket fell away and I gasped. Underneath was a pair of broken aeroplane wings. The paint was chipped and speckled with rust, and the lights on their tips were smashed. Underneath them, there appeared to be an aeroplane's tail, with a starfish painted on it in bright yellow.

"Wings!" yelled Margot, over my shoulder. She rushed over to them and traced her fingers across their surface. Her hands shook with excitement, and her mouth was open in awe. I tapped her shoulder, but she didn't notice. Margot was transfixed.

"What are they from?" I asked.

"Some sort of light aircraft. I need to find the serial number to confirm which," said Margot, her voice trembling.

"Maybe there's more of it in the next stable?" I said.

We covered the wings and tail back up, and opened the third door. Dust swirled around us like a tornado. I batted it away and blinked. An aeroplane's nose loomed up at me. Margot screamed so loudly that I was sure everyone on the mainland could hear.

"I've got to find the rest of it," she said.

"What would you do with it?" I asked.

"Rebuild it, of course," she said.

"Do you know how?"

"No, but I'll google it," replied Margot.

I could tell that she was no longer thinking about London, or phone signals, or broadband. The plane parts were too big to move, so she'd have to stay on the island if she wanted to keep them. Rebuilding a plane would keep her occupied for months, or maybe even years.

Margot started to clear the junk away from the plane's nose. I bent down to help, and picked up a stack of crispy old newspapers. A leaflet fluttered out of their pages. I picked it up and held it to the light, so I could read the faded ink.

Itchbottom Summer Festival

6th & 7th August
Music, games, stalls and sheep pageant
£10 entry

I showed the leaflet to Margot and Fabien. "Look, there's a place called Itchbottom!"

"Don't be silly," said Margot.

She peered at the leaflet, and her eyebrows arched with surprise. Fabien jumped with excitement.

"There's a sheep pageant! We've got to go," he squealed.

"That leaflet's really old," said Margot.

"They might be doing it again this year," he said.

"We should throw our own festival for ten pounds a ticket. We'd be rich!" said Margot.

"You know, that's actually not a bad idea," I told her.

"I was joking," she said.

"Yes, but just think about it," I replied. "Rebuilding your aeroplane is going to cost money, and so is opening my donkey sanctuary. This way, we could earn enough for both."

"Maybe it'll make Dad feel better," said Fabien.

"I bet it would," I replied. "Remember those

photos of him at Glastonbury when he was younger? He looked so happy in them."

"I guess it's worth a try," said Margot.

"And we could invite Mr Billionaire to thank him for the island," said Fabien.

"That's a good idea," I said. "We'll have to keep the festival a secret from Mum and Dad though. There's no way they'll let us do it if they find out. In fact, it's best not to tell them about my donkey sanctuary either."

"Or my plane," said Margot.

"Can we have a sheep pageant?" asked Fabien.

I shrugged. "It's our festival, so we can do whatever we want."

"Where would we hold it?" asked Margot.

"How about the north beach? It's out of the way enough that we can decorate it without Mum noticing," I suggested.

"All right then," said Margot. "Let's do it."

I stretched out my hand, and Margot and Fabien piled theirs on top to seal the pact. The secret festival was on.

CHAPTER
SEVEN

I was so hungry by lunchtime that even the sight of washed-up seaweed made my tummy rumble. We'd walked back to the beach after shutting up the stables, because Fabien wanted to check for buried treasure and Margot was hoping to find a cove in which she could build an aeroplane hangar. I looked towards the house and saw a wisp of smoke. Maybe Mum was cooking again.

"Look, Luna!" said Fabien, bouncing up to me. "I've found an old flip-flop, and it fits!"

"Marvellous," I said, looking at the washed-up flip-flop in his hand. "Although you have two feet, remember?"

"Yeah, I reckon the other one might be buried somewhere," he replied.

"Let's go back and get lunch before you start digging up the beach," I said.

We waved Margot over, who was in a huff because she hadn't found a cove yet, and walked back to the house. As we got closer, I realised the smoke wasn't coming from the barbecue, but from a chimney stack. I wondered what was going on. It wasn't cold enough for a fire yet, not in the daytime.

"Did you set fire to the house?" I asked Margot

suspiciously.

"Of course not! I've been with you all morning. Maybe Dad's trying to burn it down instead," she replied.

We hurried inside the house, and followed the sound of crackling logs into the living room. Soot covered the floor, and a fire roared in the hearth. It was about two thousand degrees inside the room.

"What's going on?" I asked.

"I might have dislodged a brick while I was cleaning the chimney. Just checking everything still works," said Mum. She had an old, sooty broom in one hand, and a small brick in the other.

"And does it?" asked Margot.

"Yes, I think so," replied Mum.

She threw me a duster, and a bottle of very old cleaning spray. "We need to make a start on sorting the house out. Can you three clean the bedrooms, while I tackle this room?"

"What about lunch?" I asked.

"I'll bring you something up in a minute," she replied.

Margot grabbed a big hoover from the hallway, and Fabien found a feather duster. We started with the guest bedrooms, which were tucked away in the loft. I guessed this was where Mum's yoga guests would be staying. There were three rooms, all with little round windows that looked out over the beach. Margot plugged the hoover in, and it made a *whoosh* noise, like a jumbo jet. It seemed to cheer her up.

Fabien raced through the room with his feather duster, twirling it around the lampshade as dust fell on his head, and I squirted cleaning spray on everything that didn't move. There was fresh bedding in the cupboards, zipped away in plastic storage bags. I pulled out a blanket and draped it over the bed, to make it look a bit prettier.

Mum came upstairs just as we'd finished the first bedroom, carrying a big butler's tray in front of her. I hurried over as she set it down on the newly made bed. On it were three bowls of cereal, some crackers, a lump of very warm cheese and an open tin of peaches.

"Wow, this room looks lovely," she said. "After they've all had a good lick of paint, I'll be able to charge a fortune for my yoga retreats."

I picked up a cracker. "Is this all there is to eat?"

"I got a couple of tinned steak pies yesterday,

but I thought we'd save them for dinner," said Mum.

"We really need to go food shopping properly," said Margot.

Fabien crammed a spoonful of cereal into his mouth. "Nah, this is great!"

Mum ruffled his hair. "We'll get some supplies from the mainland tomorrow."

"Where's Dad?" I said.

"I asked him to tidy our bedroom," replied Mum.

"Can I see if he wants some cheese?" I asked.

"Of course," replied Mum, and she cut a chunk off for me.

I wrapped the cheese in a napkin, and ran downstairs to Mum and Dad's new bedroom. The door was open, and Dad was sitting on the bed with his laptop beside him. I glanced around and saw a pile of dust in the corner, beside a broom. A few of his shirts hung from coat hangers in the wardrobe. It wasn't exactly the Ritz, but it looked like Dad had at least tried to clean up a little.

"What are you watching?" I asked.

He jumped and looked up at me. "What have I told you about sneaking up on people, Luna?"

"Sorry. I just thought you might want some cheese," I said, perching on the bed beside him.

He shook his head. "Thank you, but maybe later."

"Are you watching *Midsomer Murders* again?" I asked.

"Yes, it's on DVD," he replied. "Your granny was brilliant at working out who the killer was. She usually knew before the first murder."

"Can I watch it with you for a bit?" I asked.

"No, you should go and finish your lunch," he said. "I'm going to tidy a bit more anyway."

That was a good sign. I got up and headed back into the hallway, but Dad didn't move. He just sat there on the bed and continued to watch his TV show. Maybe he was going to clean more later. I thought about asking if that's what he'd meant, but my tummy rumbled, and I went upstairs instead.

Mum was sitting next to Margot, picking at the cheese and crackers. I grabbed a bowl of cereal and wondered when she'd leave. I wanted to talk to Margot and Fabien about our festival, but I couldn't do it in front of her. We needed to start making a plan, and didn't have any time to lose.

"I think if we all pitch in to clean your bedrooms we ought to finish by teatime," said Mum.

"Can't we do it tomorrow?" I asked.

"Best to do them today, while we're in the zone," replied Mum.

I groaned. Cleaning our bedrooms would take the rest of the afternoon. I guessed planning our festival would have to wait until tomorrow.

CHAPTER EIGHT

"We'll need a stage, and a band to put on the stage," said Margot the next morning.

I curled my toes in the sand. "Fabien can sing."

"We can't charge people ten pounds to come and hear Fabien. We need a band, or somebody famous," said Margot.

"All right, we'll put an advert in the local paper," I said.

"What if Mum reads it? I thought we were keeping the festival a secret," said Margot.

"We are. You know she only reads the paper when it's wrapped around chips," I said.

"That's true," replied Margot.

As if her ears were burning, Mum appeared from the trees behind us with Fabien. There was no sign of Dad. She waved at us, and untied *Lady Agatha* from her mooring, ready for our supplies trip to the mainland. My tummy flipped nervously at how she'd almost overheard us. We'd need to be careful with planning the festival. It was much better to tell her about it on the day, when it was too late to cancel. Besides, it was more likely to cheer Dad up if it was a surprise.

I jumped into the boat behind the others, and we sped away from our island. Mum let me steer for a bit, and we weaved our way past fishing boats, lazy seagulls and a yacht. Margot studied the computer system, and Fabien waved at everyone we passed from beneath his deerstalker hat. It was a bit different from our usual tube ride.

Before long, we reached the harbour and I leapt off the boat. The first person I saw was Kai. He was in the window of The Wig and Pen, sticking something to the inside of the glass. I waved, but he scowled back and turned away. He definitely didn't like us. I wondered what we'd done to upset him.

"Can I use The Wig and Pen's Internet?" I asked Mum.

"Me too!" said Margot.

"All right," replied Mum. "I need to go to the butcher's first, so go straight inside and I'll meet you in there."

"I want to go to the butcher's too!" said Fabien, who liked to picket their shops, shouting anti-lamb-eating slogans.

Margot and I waved goodbye to Mum, and opened the door to The Wig and Pen. I stood in the entrance and gawped. Every surface was covered with slices of Victoria sponge,

Battenberg and chocolate eclairs. Half the village seemed to be there too, buried up to their necks in crumbs, and licking icing from their lips. It was like a natural disaster movie, but the tsunami was made of cake.

"Are you here for the Cakeathon?" asked Heidi, who was halfway through munching a slice of Swiss roll.

"What's a Cakeathon?" I asked.

"We're raising money for charity by eating cake," she said. "Can I tempt you to a slice of lemon drizzle?"

"Oh, no, thank you," I said.

I made a beeline for the computer, and was almost there when a lady sprang out at me from behind a pile of red-velvet cupcakes. "Daisy Gifford, editor-in-chief of the *Wishnook Gazette*," she said, waving a hand at me.

"Um … hello," I replied.

"Any quote for me?" she asked.

"Excuse me?" said Margot.

Heidi got up and steered the woman away from us. "Please excuse Daisy. News is a little slow around here, so your arrival is front-page material."

"We don't want to be in the paper," I said.

"Nobody really does. That's the problem," replied Daisy.

I smiled at her awkwardly, and edged away to the computer. Maybe advertising for bands in the newspaper wasn't such a good idea after all. Something told me Daisy Gifford wasn't the type of person who could keep a secret.

The Wig and Pen's computer groaned into life. I waited about ten years for it to start up, and then began to google photos of festivals. Margot made a note beside me of all the things we needed, from bunting to speakers. The list got longer and longer.

"It's going to cost a fortune to even put on the festival," said Margot.

"Not if we make everything ourselves," I said.

"How are we going to make a stage?" asked Margot.

"There must be instructions somewhere," I replied.

Sure enough, the first website I clicked on had a step-by-step guide to making a stage. It wasn't a big one, but was just tall enough to raise a band above people's heads. I printed it off and highlighted all the things we needed: a few pallets, a box of nails and a couple of screws. The whole thing looked pretty easy. A lick of black paint and I bet none of the visitors would know we hadn't bought it.

"Now all we need to do is find some wood," I said.

Heidi sashayed over to the bar, and glanced at the instructions in my hands. "Building something?"

"A bat house," I lied, covering the diagrams.

"Oh, how sweet! Well, the McAndrews always have spare pallets," she said, scraping a piece of chocolate cake on to a plate. "Tell you what, I'll ask Kai to take you there when he delivers their newspaper tomorrow."

I didn't know whether to feel excited or sick. "Really? I don't think Kai likes us very much."

"Nonsense!" Heidi laughed. "Kai likes everyone."

As if by magic, Kai appeared from behind the bar. I smiled at him, but he ducked behind a pile of banana bread to avoid my gaze. Heidi was wrong; Kai definitely didn't like everyone, or at least not me.

Before I could say anything, the door tinkled open and Mum entered, followed by some kind of large, fluffy lump. It looked like a werewolf crossed with a rug. I narrowed my eyes in concentration, and tried to work out what it was. A pair of trainers stuck out of the bottom of the strange thing, and I recoiled in horror. The trainers belonged to my brother.

Margot glanced over, and her face went pink with embarrassment.

"I found a sheep costume in the charity shop!" Fabien announced, twirling around.

The costume was at least three sizes too big, and hung off his shoulders like a tent. It was made of real matted wool, which looked like it needed a good wash. There was a pair of pointy ears on Fabien's head, and a button attached to his nose with elastic. It was like he'd rolled around in a bag of cotton balls.

"I'm going to fool the goats into thinking I'm one of them!" he said.

"Won't they realise you're a sheep?" I asked.

"Won't they realise you're a *person*?" muttered Margot.

"No, because I'm going to do my very best

goat impression," said Fabien.

He knelt down and bounded across the floor towards me. I screamed as he bumped into a table and an avalanche of fondant fancies fell on his head. He leapt up, startled, and collided with a fruit cake. It sailed through the air and landed on the end of a cake slice, which spun across the room, smashed into a chocolate cake and splattered icing all over Kai.

Daisy Gifford's camera lit up the room with a series of excited flashes.

I groaned, and buried my head in my hands. If Kai hadn't already hated us, then he definitely did now. Our trip tomorrow was going to be torture.

CHAPTER

NINE

I met Kai outside The Wig and Pen the next morning, while Mum sat inside and tried to create a website for her yoga retreat. It was just me and him, because Margot had decided to stay on the island and work on her plane, while Fabien crafted a goat shelter from an old anorak. I hoped the trip wouldn't take long.

Kai was leaning against two bicycles, one covered in mud, and the other in painted flowers. He waved a newspaper at me. My face was on its front page.

"You're famous," he muttered.

I took the paper from him and read the headline: *New Family Move to Rook's Island and Cause Havoc!* It went on to explain how we'd won the island, and to describe how Fabien, dressed as a sheep, had destroyed the Cakeathon in a matter of thirty seconds. The word "bonkers" was used several times.

"That's so unfair!" I exclaimed. "Can't we sue her or something?"

"She's not lying," replied Kai.

I threw the newspaper back at him, and prayed Margot would never see it.

Kai climbed on to the muddy bike, and pointed

me towards the flowery one. It was huge, and the frame was bent in the middle. I stared at it, and tried to remember the last time I'd ridden a bike.

It took me a few seconds to get the hang of balancing, and I had to lean on the wall to steady myself. Mum and Dad had never let us cycle in London. They'd made us walk everywhere, even though Margot had once argued that it was child abuse.

"Ready?" asked Kai, but he set off before I could answer.

I pressed my feet to the pedals, and zigzagged after him. The morning fish market was in full swing down at the harbour, and the village was busier than I'd seen it before. Tables of salmon and crab stretched across the shore, and the smell of them made my eyes water. People shouted prices and weights over the sound of jingling money belts. It was so different from the supermarket next to our old flat.

We reached the edge of the village, and the market petered out. The road snaked uphill, and I fumbled around with the gears. My legs felt like they were made of stone.

"Race you!" said Kai.

He tore up the hill, and left me in a swirl of dust. I gripped the handlebars, and pressed my toes hard against the pedals. The wheels went *click, click, click* beneath me. I gritted my teeth, determined to catch him. Kai was testing me to see if I could keep up. I'd show him.

My wheels drew level with Kai's, and he eased up on the pedals. I slumped over my handlebars and tried to catch my breath. My heart drummed quickly and I wished I could hide how exhausted I was.

"Not bad for a city rat," said Kai.

"It's easy to keep up with a country slug," I replied.

"Slugs have more teeth than sharks," said Kai. "You shouldn't annoy them."

I couldn't tell if he was being serious or not, but didn't want to ask.

Kai sped off again, and I pedalled after him. Soon the coast disappeared, and all I could see were green fields. They rolled into the distance for miles and miles. Every direction looked the same, and my stomach churned. If Kai left me now, I'd have no idea how to get back to the village. I'd be lost.

A farmhouse appeared in the distance. Kai swung his bike down a gravel road, and I hurried to keep up with him. Smoke mushroomed into the sky, and I caught a whiff of burnt wood. This must be it.

"I hope they're not burning the pallets!" I said.

"What do you want them for anyway?" asked Kai.

"I'm building something," I replied.

He narrowed his eyes at me. "What sort of something?"

"Why are you so interested?" I asked.

"Because you're going to mess everything up!" he snapped.

"Mess what up?" I said, bewildered.

"The island. My dad used to take care of it for Mr Harding. He made sure the cliffs were clear of rubbish so the seals could breed there, and the bats had enough shelter, and the trees didn't starve the other plants of light. He kept the house clean, and repaired the mooring, and stopped the pipes freezing in winter," explained Kai.

"Well, he didn't do a very good job, because the house is full of bats, and the stables are covered in vines and full of rubbish," I said.

Kai slowed down and looked at his pedals. "Well, it was a bit hard for him to keep on top of it after he died."

I wanted the ground to swallow me up whole. "I'm sorry… I didn't know."

"Dad loved that island, and now you're going to build things on it and ruin it all," he said.

"I'm not!" I replied. "I need the pallets to build a stage for a festival, so I can raise money to open a donkey sanctuary. I love the island, and the bats, and the plants. I don't want to ruin them."

Kai stopped pedalling and stared hard at me, as if trying to decide whether I was telling the truth. Now it all made sense. The reason Kai had been so unfriendly was that the island reminded him of his dad. Maybe he was worried that we'd change it from the place his dad had loved. After Granny died, the council had said we had to clear out her flat so somebody else could live there. The place looked so different afterwards, like she'd never even existed. I guessed Kai felt the same way about the island.

"My granny died a few months ago, and my dad started acting really differently afterwards," I said. "He just lies in bed and sleeps all day.

We thought having a festival might give him something to smile about." I wasn't sure why I was telling him all of this. It felt good to talk to somebody other than Margot and Fabien about it, but embarrassing too.

Kai turned away from me, scuffed the ground with his shoe and then pulled back his shoulders. "We'd better get going, before Farmer McAndrew burns all the wood."

I looked back to the smoke-filled sky, and pedalled towards it in a panic. A huge bonfire danced in the middle of a gravel courtyard, its flames orange and fierce. Beside it, a man in a tweed jacket threw something into the flames. The fire crackled hungrily and the smoke thickened. I guessed the man was Farmer McAndrew.

We screeched to a halt in front of him, and Kai handed him his newspaper.

"This is Luna," said Kai, gesturing to me. "She's after some old pallets for a project."

"There's half a dozen or so behind the cow-shed," said Farmer McAndrew. "Help yourself, just don't disturb my girls."

"Girls?" I whispered, but Kai was already halfway across the courtyard.

I cycled after him to a field full of large tan-coloured cows. They didn't look anything like the cute spotty ones I was used to seeing in milk adverts. These were dumb and angry looking, and smelled like the inside of a train-station toilet.

"Not scared, are you?" asked Kai.

"Of course not!" I lied.

"Good. Come on then," he said.

I took a deep breath, and followed Kai through the gate. My wheels clicked over the grass, and all the cows stopped chewing and glared up at me. It was as if they could smell my fear.

They're just like donkeys; they're just like donkeys, I said to myself, but didn't feel any calmer.

I skirted past the cows, and cycled as fast as I could to the other side of the field. Kai stopped at the shed, and laughed over his shoulder at me. He was about to say something, but then suddenly his face turned pale and his eyes widened. I skidded to a halt, and tried to spot what he was looking at.

"The gate!" he yelled.

"What gate?" I asked.

"The gate!" he repeated.

I looked back at the gate to the field, and saw it swing open in the breeze. The cows stampeded towards it, tails swishing. Hot panic filled me. I must have forgotten to close it when I'd followed Kai through.

"Quick, we've got to stop them!" he said.

My wheels spun as I pedalled back across the field. Mud splattered my back and my wheels tore up the grass. It was too late. The entire herd was loose.

I watched in horror as the cows almost crashed into Farmer McAndrew, veered left and ploughed through his vegetable patch. Cabbage leaves and cucumbers flew through the air, and an onion landed on the garage roof. One of the cows collided with a watering can and got its foot stuck inside. It clattered around like a one-cow band, and water sloshed out of the top.

"We need to stop them before they leave the farm!" yelled Kai.

I forced myself to cycle faster. The cows crashed through a plastic washing line, sending a pair of blanket-sized knickers into the air. I watched the knickers parachute down and land on one of the cows' head, covering its eyes. The cow mooed loudly, and fell into a pile of manure. I choked on the smell.

Kai got in front of the cows and waved his arms at them. They stampeded towards him without blinking. My breath caught in my chest. Kai was going to be flattened.

"Moo at them!" he yelled.

"Are you mad?" I asked.

"Do you want me to be roadkill?" he said.

Before I could properly think about it, I sucked in a deep breath and let out an almighty moo. The cows screeched to a halt and stared at me. I gripped my handlebars and stared back. Nobody moved. It was like a standoff in an old Western.

Farmer McAndrew ran past me and shook a bucket of food at the cows. They blinked, mooed and trotted after it. My heart drummed in my ears. I couldn't believe what had just happened.

"Let's get out of here," said Kai.

"But what about my stage?" I asked.

"Hang around here and it won't just be wood that Farmer McAndrew's burning," he said.

I glanced back at the pallets, and then cycled away as if my life depended on it. We didn't stop until we reached The Wig and Pen. I clambered off the bike, and wheeled it over to Kai. He grabbed the handlebars without scowling at me, and I wondered if maybe we were friends now. It would be nice to know somebody other than Margot and Fabien.

"Do you want a can of pop?" he asked.

That was definitely the type of question you'd ask a friend, I thought. "Yes, please," I smiled.

I followed Kai inside. Mum was still sitting at the computer. I went over to see what she was doing, while Kai fetched the drinks. On the computer screen was a website, with a photo of our beach at the top, and random people doing yoga poses below.

"What do you think?" asked Mum.

"It's very good," I replied, surprised.

"Heidi helped me a bit," said Mum.

Just then, Kai came over and handed me a can of lemonade. "What's that?" he asked.

Mum explained all about her yoga retreat idea. "Hopefully we'll be able to save up enough money to renovate the house, if the business takes off. I might even be able to build a yoga studio so I can teach classes during winter, and maybe some log cabins so we can have even more guests."

"You mean like a holiday park?" asked Kai.

"Well … yes, I suppose a bit like that," said Mum.

I had a bad feeling about where this chat was heading. Kai's face had gone hard and stormy. It was like he was trying to kill me with his glare.

"You liar," he said to me.

"I'm not a liar!" I said.

"You said you weren't going to build on the island!" he said.

"We're not!" I replied but, before I could say anything else, Kai stomped off upstairs.

I sank into the chair next to Mum and groaned. So much for Kai and I being friends. Now he *really* didn't like us.

"Oh, dear… Did I cause that?" asked Mum.

"You're not really going to build all that stuff, are you? It'll ruin the island," I said, thinking mostly about my donkey sanctuary. There'd be no room for it if Mum covered the island with log cabins. The yoga people would scare all the animals away, including my donkeys.

"It was just an idea," said Mum. "I doubt we'd actually be able to afford it, and I suppose it *would* be a lot of work. Maybe you're right and it would spoil things. I was just thinking aloud."

I sipped my lemonade with relief. My donkey sanctuary was still safe then. Now all I had to worry about was Kai. I couldn't believe I'd told him about the festival. What if he tried to ruin it, or told Mum about it? Margot and Fabien were going to kill me.

CHAPTER

TEN

The next morning, Fabien handed me a leaflet. It was an advert for this year's festival in Itchbottom, which he'd picked up from The Wig and Pen before the Cakeathon incident. According to the dates, the festival was that day.

"We could ask to borrow their stage," said Fabien, who was sitting on the floor, trying to find the town on a map.

"I doubt they'll lend it to us," I said, throwing my head into my hands mournfully.

"Can't we go anyway? I want to see the sheep," said Fabien.

Margot nodded. "It'd be good research at least."

I got up and accidentally stood on the top of Scotland, but Fabien shooed me off so he could highlight the roads to Itchbottom. The town didn't look very far from our island, just a couple of centimetres. I wondered if the map was to scale.

"You get Mum and Dad, and I'll get my costume," said Fabien, bouncing up from the sofa.

Margot shook her head frantically. "No! You can't go to a sheep show dressed as a sheep!"

"Why not?" asked Fabien.

"Because it's like going to a music festival dressed as a trombone!" she said.

"That would be funny," giggled Fabien, and went to fetch his costume regardless.

Margot breathed a long, deep, pitiful sigh.

I told Mum about the Itchbottom festival over a breakfast of burnt eels, while Fabien groomed his coat. She was so surprised that we'd managed to read a map that she barely protested at the idea of going, although Dad was harder to convince. We had to drag the covers off him and pull a jumper over his head before he'd even sit up. Eventually we managed to cajole him into *Lady Agatha*, where he sat quietly in the corner.

Itchbottom was twenty miles and two bus rides away. I sat by the window of each one and kept watch for our stop. The journey took less than an hour, but it felt like days. I fidgeted in my seat, and wiggled my thumbs impatiently.

"How much further?" asked Fabien.

"Not far," I said.

"I'm hungry," he replied.

I tossed him a satsuma. "We can eat when we get there."

The bus wobbled around a bend, and we passed a sign saying *Welcome to Itchbottom. Twinned with Scratchbottom in Memphis.* Ahead was a bus stop covered in posters. I tried to read them, but couldn't make out the writing. One had a drawing of a sheep on it.

"Let's get off here," I said.

The bus doors swooshed open. I stepped outside and smelled fried onions and burgers. There was a cheer in the distance, and the muffled sound of a megaphone.

Fabien screamed, "THE SHEEP PAGEANT IS HAPPENING IN TEN MINUTES!"

"What?" we all asked him.

He pointed to a poster plastered to the bus shelter. According to the schedule, Itchbottom's Most Glamorous Sheep Pageant was due to start at midday, directly followed by a special appearance from Carlos, the multi-prizewinning, internationally renowned Rasa Aragonesa sheep.

Before I had even finished reading the rest of the line-up, a girl ran past us with a lamb in her arms. Fabien's eyes bulged and he nearly toppled over with excitement. I reached out to grab him, but he darted after the lamb in a trembling blur.

Margot shook her head. "I really wish he wasn't wearing that outfit."

We caught up with Fabien at the gates of a park. Hundreds of people were on the other side, and in the middle of them was a show ring. Margot and I each grabbed one of Fabien's arms, and held on to him tightly. He was so excited, I thought he might faint.

Fabien struggled against us. "Come on! I need to get a good spot."

We pushed our way to the front of the show ring, where the rams were already warming up. I stared at them and burst out laughing. Some were in waistcoats, and others little jumpers. A couple had ribbons twined in their fur, two had flowers on their heads and one was wearing a giant sombrero.

"They're so handsome!" cried Fabien.

A lady inside the show ring spotted us and grinned. She had a clipboard and looked very official.

"Are you entering your ram into the contest?" she said, winking at Fabien.

It was obviously a joke, but Fabien twisted away from us and ran into the ring. Margot and

I exchanged horrified glances. Behind us, Mum made a squeaking noise. I couldn't tell if she was embarrassed or proud.

"It's just a bit of fun," said the woman, who I now realised was the judge.

I shuffled my feet uncomfortably as the contest started. Fabien lined up with the real sheep, and they took it in turns to prance around the ring. The crowd cheered loudly as the first started its lap. It trotted around gracefully, and then pulled free of its handler and jumped out of the ring. I gasped as it collided with a candyfloss stall, and a nest of pink sugar fluttered on to its head. The crowd erupted into fits of hysterical laughter.

Fabien was the last "sheep" to move. He skipped around the ring, baaing, and waved at the audience. Beside me, Margot lowered her head in shame.

The judge signalled for silence, and chewed her pen as she considered the motley line-up. A drum roll sounded. I closed my eyes and prayed that the grass would swallow me up.

Please don't let it be Fabien; please don't let it be Fabien, I thought.

"And the winner is…"

There was a dramatic pause, punctuated only by a chorus of *baas*.

"Mr Blanket!" she announced.

The crowd cheered, and Mr Blanket, the winning sheep, did a victory prance around the ring.

"And this year, we're giving an honourable mention to young Fabien," continued the judge, sticking a rosette on his forehead.

I groaned. My brother had actually just won a prize in a sheep beauty pageant. It was possibly the most embarrassing moment of my life.

Margot turned to me. "We can never tell anyone about this."

"Agreed," I replied.

We slipped away from the crowd and did a circuit of the festival, while Fabien basked in the glow of his achievement. Mum and Dad sat on a bench, sipping lemonade. Dad gave me a small wave, and tapped his finger against his glass in time to the music as the band started to play. It was the most alive I'd seen him look in weeks. I squeezed Margot's hand. Our dad was still in there somewhere.

Fabien danced past me. I buried my embarrassed face in a notebook, and scribbled down everything I could see. There was a vegetarian burger van, a hot-dog stand, a doughnut vendor and a candyfloss stall. Behind the show ring was a stage with two large speakers and coloured disco balls. It looked much fancier than the one I'd found instructions to build. There was a microphone and everything.

Dozens of stalls were scattered around the festival field, their tables piled with things to buy. There were woven bracelets, colourful hats and temporary tattoos. A lady sat on the floor with a palette of face paints, and another was braiding people's hair.

I swallowed hard. The festival was much bigger than I'd expected. I wondered how Margot and I would ever be able to organise our own.

Margot's phone buzzed in her pocket, and she leapt into the air with shocked excitement. I didn't recognise the number on the screen. Margot answered anyway.

"Hello?"

There was a pause, as whoever was calling said something to her, and then she nodded down the phone. "Brilliant. I'll see you tomorrow at 3 p.m. then."

"Who was that?" I asked.

"That was a band wanting to audition for our festival," she replied. "I put up an advert in the window of The Wig and Pen the other day."

"But what if Mum sees it?" I asked.

"There's no way she'll know it's our advert. I didn't mention the island; I just said it was a local festival," said Margot.

"Oh, OK then," I replied. Margot was quite good at all this covert stuff. "What's the band like?"

Margot shrugged. "No idea, but I guess we'll find out tomorrow."

CHAPTER
ELEVEN

The garage next to The Wig and Pen was also its function room. It was just big enough to squeeze me, Margot, Fabien and a three-piece band inside. Heidi had let us use it in return for cleaning her windows while Mum was visiting the mobile bank and Dad was in his usual spot under the duvet.

I sat down next to Fabien, who appraised the band. They shuffled uncomfortably under his gaze, and I heard one of their backs creak.

"Just how old *are* you exactly?" asked Fabien.

"Fabien!" hissed Margot.

The leader of the band chuckled. "I'm Frank, seventy-six, Joe here is eighty, and Gwen is a mere sixty-three."

"Wow," I mouthed. They weren't exactly what I'd imagined for our festival. I wondered if Dad would like them.

"And do you play anything besides the trumpet?" asked Fabien.

"Trombone," corrected Frank. "And, yes, I also play the guitar."

"Good. Can we hear that instead?" asked Fabien.

Frank put down his trombone, picked up a

guitar from the corner and counted the others in. Joe dragged his fingers across his washboard, and Gwen pursed her lips on her flute. The weirdest version I'd ever heard of "We Will Rock You" filled the garage.

My foot tapped along as The Rocking Pensioners played. It was kind of good in a weird way. They had my vote.

Fabien raised his hand. "I think we need something for the younger audience."

"Who *are* you?" asked Margot, blinking at our brother.

"I'm being Simon Cowell," he said. "Do you want to swap for a bit?"

Margot scraped her chair over to me and whispered, "Do you think people will pay to listen to them?"

"We've still got another band to audition after this," I said. "These could be the warm-up act."

Fabien Cowell nodded. "They could be good with some work."

"OK, you're hired," I told them.

"Figuratively speaking," said Margot. "We can't actually pay you."

"We don't want your money, dear," said Gwen.

"We play because we have rock 'n' roll in our soul."

"Yes, and it keeps our joints from seizing up," added Frank.

"Oh, well, that's great then," replied Margot.

"When did you say the festival was again?" asked Frank.

"Um…" I said.

Margot and I stared at each other. We'd been so busy thinking about the band and the stage that we hadn't actually come up with a date. It was already the first week of August. In less than a month, summer would be over, and there'd be no point in having a festival during winter. I needed the money to fix my stables now, while the weather was still good, and the days still light.

"The last Saturday of the month," said Margot.

I counted the weeks on my fingers. There were only two weekends between now and then. My hands sweated at the thought of getting everything ready in time.

The Rocking Pensioners nodded, and started to pack up their instruments.

"Should we confirm with your parents?" asked Gwen.

"No!" said Margot. "I mean, no, there's no need. We're in charge of entertainment."

"Our mum's busy sorting her yoga retreat out," I said.

"Yes, so she's getting us to do the band auditions," added Margot.

"Oh ... righty-ho," said Gwen.

I stared at Margot and whispered, "You're a genius sometimes, do you know that?"

The next band entered as the pensioners were leaving. They were a good forty years younger than Gwen. Thankfully there wasn't a trombone in sight.

Margot stared at the lead singer and smiled dreamily. He had a ukulele strung around his neck. It looked a bit like a shrunken guitar. I kicked Margot under the table, but she didn't even blink.

"I'm Brice," said the boy.

"Brice," she repeated softly.

"Yes, Brice," he nodded.

"Brice," she breathed again.

"OK, Margot, I think we know his name now," I said, and then I turned to Fabien. "Can you please go and keep a lookout for Mum? I think this might take a while."

"All right, but you'll be begging me to come back for the next episode," he said.

"We're not on TV," I called after him.

Brice and his band, which turned out to be called Brice and Brothers, started strumming on their ukuleles and singing. Margot clapped and cheered along, like they were The Beatles. Halfway through, Brice dropped his ukulele and broke into a rap. I could practically see Margot's heart fluttering through her chest.

"Wonderful! I love you!" she exclaimed at the end. "I mean, we love you. Your music, that is."

"Oh, cool," said Brice, and he scribbled the date of the festival down on a napkin.

I waited for the band to leave, and then turned to Margot. "You looooove him," I teased.

"Do not," replied Margot.

"You want to marry him," I sang.

"Shut up, Luna," she said.

I started humming the "Wedding March" but then the door opened again and someone stepped inside. Margot thrust her hand over my mouth and tackled me to the ground before I could see who it was. I wriggled free and hoped it wasn't Brice. She'd never forgive me if he'd overheard.

Luckily it was just Kai.

"What is it with your family and rolling around on the floor?" he asked.

I struggled back into my chair, red faced. "We … tripped. Anyway, what are you doing here? Your mum said we could use the room."

"I've come to audition," he said.

"Audition for what?" I replied.

"Fabien told me you're holding auditions for the festival today," he said, and he stood on the gaffer-taped X that Fabien had stuck to the floor. "So, can I audition, or what?"

"But you haven't got any instruments," I said.

"Don't need them," he replied, and he opened his mouth and started singing.

I stood up, ready to tell Kai that he was awful and to go away. The only problem was, he wasn't. He might not have had a guitar, or a flute, or a ukulele, but he sounded far better than Frank's and Brice's bands put together. I leaned back in my chair, annoyed. The last person I wanted to perform at our festival was Kai. He'd probably refuse to turn up on the day, just to sabotage it.

"Well?" he asked, when he'd finished. For a

second he looked kind of nervous.

Margot applauded. "That was really good, wasn't it, Luna?"

"It was all right," I muttered.

"So, can I be in the festival?" he asked.

"Why do you want to? You hate us," I said.

"I like singing," he said. "And this way I can make sure you don't chop down the woods and turn the island into a camping site."

I wasn't sure if we could trust him or not, but he *was* a good singer, and the more performers we had, the better.

"All right then," I replied, slowly.

I really hoped it wasn't a trap.

CHAPTER

TWELVE

"I've got my first booking!" exclaimed Mum, back at the island that afternoon.

I flopped a fish on to the barbecue. "For what?"

"For my yoga retreat, of course," she replied.

"For when?" I asked.

"Next weekend. It's a group of five ladies and two men," said Mum.

I plucked a blade of grass from our front lawn, and pinched it apart with my fingers. What if the yoga guests found out about the festival? It would be difficult to get everything ready with a bunch of strangers nosing around.

Margot hammered a nail into the bat box she'd been building, and stood back to admire it. "I'll move the bats' new roost into the woods."

"Are you sure next weekend isn't a bit soon?" I asked Mum. "Wouldn't it be better if they came in September? Or maybe even October?"

"I'm sure I can be ready by next week," replied Mum. "Money's getting a bit tight, so the sooner they come the better. Otherwise we'll be eating offal and seaweed for the next month."

Fabien wrinkled his nose. "That sounds vile."

After lunch, Mum put us in charge of decorating the guest bedrooms. I found a load of leftover paint under the stairs, and sploshed a tin called Sapphire Ducks into a tray. Margot nodded approvingly and said it reminded her of one of the oceans in her flight simulator.

Dad poked his head inside the room, and for a moment I thought he'd got lost.

"Is there a spare paintbrush?" he asked.

Fabien bounced over to him. "You can help me paint the bottom bits if you want," he said.

I couldn't believe it. Dad was actually helping! Maybe he'd finally realised how brilliant the island was, and was starting to feel better. I knew it would fix everything.

Dad smeared a line of paint on to the wall. It took him ages to do one tiny patch. He kept going over and over it, until the bristles were clean. About five minutes later, he creaked to his feet and passed me the brush.

"You kids are doing a great job," he said.

"Are you finished?" I asked.

"I'm a little tired," he replied, and then he disappeared down the landing.

Fabien put down his paintbrush with a sigh. "I'm going to make some curtains."

Margot and I carried on painting until the

entire room was a shimmering blue. I stood back to admire our work. It looked really good, and perfect for guests.

Fabien came back into the room with an armful of knitting, which I assumed was the start of his curtains. It was the colour of mushy peas, and kind of reminded me of vomit.

"What do you think?" asked Fabien. "Obviously they'll be a lot bigger when they're finished."

"It's … um … lovely," lied Margot.

"Green is very fashionable in knitwear this year," said Fabien. "I want to dye the goats lime-coloured when I tame them." And he bounded off to go and feed them.

Two days later, Mum showed us a list of things she needed for the retreat, like bed sheets, and beach towels, and battery-powered speakers. I pondered the list as we sped to the mainland. If only Amazon delivered to our island.

"You three look for the items at the top of the list, and I'll get the last four," said Mum.

I tore the list in half, and headed to the charity shop with Margot and Fabien. The lady behind the counter jumped when we entered. I handed over the list, and she whirled around, digging under piles of dusty clothes, books and mugs. The shelves were bursting with decades' worth of donations that had gone unsold and unloved. I wouldn't have been surprised if there'd been a stage somewhere underneath it all. She seemed to have every other item imaginable.

The lady returned five minutes later with everything on our list. I crammed them inside a giant carrier bag while Margot paid, and then dragged the bag outside on to the high street. Mission accomplished.

"Let's go to the park," said Fabien, now we had time to kill.

I followed him along the street but, halfway up, something caught my eye. Outside the mechanic's shop was an ice-cream van, rusty, dented and covered in mud. It looked so uncared for that I wondered whether it had been abandoned.

"Look, ice cream!" exclaimed Fabien.

Margot peered inside the van's side window. "I wonder if it still works."

My heart raced. The ice-cream van would be perfect for the festival. Maybe whoever owned it would sell it to us. And afterwards we could have ice cream whenever we wanted!

I poked my head into the garage and called out, "Hello, anybody in?"

A pair of legs slid out from underneath a car, followed by a torso and then a head.

"Can I help you?" he asked.

"Do you know if anyone owns the ice-cream van outside?" I said.

The man nodded. "Yes, she's mine."

"Oh. Any chance you want to sell her?" I asked.

"No, I'm going to turn her into a camper," he replied.

"Doesn't it work then?"

"She'll go for about two minutes at a time, but then the engine cuts out. Got another month before the replacement arrives," he sighed.

Margot came over to us, and sat down on a tyre. "What about the ice-cream-maker part?"

"Oh, yes, that works a treat, if you'll excuse the pun," he replied.

"Do you think we could maybe borrow it for a couple of weeks?" I asked.

He laughed. "You want to borrow my van?"

I wondered whether to tell him about the festival. It seemed like the only way to explain why we wanted the van. Besides, we'd have to start telling people about it sooner or later, or nobody would turn up. I just hoped he wouldn't bump into Mum beforehand and spill the beans.

"A festival, eh?" he replied.

Margot nodded. "The Rocking Pensioners are playing, and Brice and Brothers, and Kai's singing."

The man looked excited. "I love Frank's band! I'm their biggest fan."

"Really? So does that mean we can borrow the van?" I asked. "We'll give you all the free ice cream you want, and make sure you're right at the front of the stage for when Frank's on."

"All right, I can't see any harm in it," he said.

I leapt into the air, and then hugged the bonnet of the van. Now all we had to do was get it to our island. My heart sank as a terrible realisation hit me. We needed Kai's help.

"Can you distract Mum for a bit? I need to talk to Kai," I told Margot and Fabien.

"What are you going to say to him?" asked Margot.

I had no idea, but I had to think of something. We needed that ice-cream van.

CHAPTER THIRTEEN

I sat down on the beach near the harbour, and grabbed a handful of pebbles. How was I going to convince Kai to help us? Maybe I could trick him and Doug into shipping the ice-cream van to our island. Anything was worth a try.

A bird squawked in the distance and I glanced up. Out at sea, a gull was thrashing about on the water. It had probably caught a fish or something. I put my sunglasses on and looked at it properly. The bird had something wrapped around its body, pinning down one of its wings. A wave rose up behind him, and the bird struggled to stay afloat. It was in trouble.

The bird was about fifty metres away from the harbour. I looked around, but there was nobody nearby to help. I had to do something, or the bird would drown. It was up to me to save it.

Without thinking, I kicked off my trainers and ran into the sea. The stones dug into my feet, and the cold water numbed my toes. I winced and carried on, until the water was up to my waist. A big wave rose up behind the bird again, and it disappeared beneath the surface for a few seconds. My tummy lurched, and I threw the rest of my body into the sea.

A wave rolled towards me, and I kicked hard against it. The bird slipped under the water again. I kept going, until I realised that I couldn't see the bottom of the sea any more. My heart thumped fast, but I couldn't stop now. I had to keep going.

Finally, I reached the bird, and grabbed it with my hands. Its free wing flapped fiercely against me, and I tucked it up close to my neck. Swimming was much harder with only one arm. I panted as I headed back to shore, my legs getting heavier. At least I wasn't pushing against the waves any more, though, and each one helped to sweep me along, until finally I could stand again.

I staggered out of the water, and knelt down on the shore. The pebbles dug into my legs, but I didn't care. I was just happy to see dry land again, and so was the bird. It scrabbled out of my arms, and then collapsed in a heap next to me. I bent over and tried to catch my breath. The bird opened its beak wide and panted. I wasn't sure who was more shocked.

A pair of boots appeared in front of me, and I looked up. There, towering above my head, was Kai. He stared from me, to the bird, and then back again.

"What's going on?" he asked.

"It was drowning," I said, sitting back on my heels and turning to the bird.

Kai knelt down beside me, and scooped the bird on to his lap. I leaned over him and inspected the thing wrapped around its wing and body. It was some sort of plastic wrap, like cling film, only thicker. It must have been floating in the water, and snaked around the seagull when it landed. Without both its wings, the bird hadn't been able to fly off again.

I found the end of the plastic and gently began to unravel it. Kai lifted the bird as I worked, and soon the bird was free. He set it down on the beach, and I waited for it to fly off. Instead, the poor thing just lay there, eyes wide.

"What's wrong with him?" I asked.

"He's in shock," said Kai.

"Will he be OK?" I asked.

"I don't know. He needs somewhere quiet and safe to recover," said Kai.

"You could put him in one of your rabbit cages until he feels better," I said.

"Good idea," he replied.

I wrung out the bottoms of my jeans. "Do you

have a towel? Mum will kill me if she sees I've been in the water alone."

"What were you doing out there?" asked Kai.

"I saw the bird was in trouble," I said.

"And you swam out to rescue him?" asked Kai, as if he didn't believe me.

"Yes, I'm a good swimmer," I replied.

"You should never go in the sea on your own. You could get swept out by the current, or hit by an incoming boat. You have to be careful of the ocean. It's not like a swimming pool," said Kai.

"I didn't think of that," I said. "Anyway, what do you care? I thought you hated me."

"That doesn't mean I want you to drown," he replied. "You should never do that again."

"OK, I promise," I said.

"Good. Come with me and I'll get you a towel," he replied.

I followed Kai back to The Wig and Pen, and he settled the seagull into an empty rabbit cage in the corner of the garden. It lay at the back, still as a statue. For a minute, I wondered if it was still alive, and then it shuffled a little.

Kai threw a towel at me, and unpegged one of his mum's tops from the line. I ducked behind the shed to get changed, and ruffled my hair with the towel. Suddenly I felt much warmer, and a little less shaky.

"Where are your sister and brother?" asked Kai, when I emerged from behind the shed.

I hung my old top over his washing line. "They're distracting Mum while I came to ask you something."

"Me?" he asked.

"We need a favour," I replied. "And I know you don't like us, but I was hoping that maybe you might help us anyway."

"What is it?" he asked.

I explained how we'd found the ice-cream van, and how we needed a way to get it to the island. Kai sat on the back step of The Wig and Pen, and listened quietly. I couldn't tell what he was thinking.

"We're not planning to turn the island into a scrapyard, or open an ice-cream factory on it, or hold ice-cream-van rallies," I said, before he could ask anything. "It's just for a couple of days, as something nice for the festival. And I promise this isn't part of some plan to turn the island into a holiday resort, because my mum wasn't being serious about that."

I took a deep breath, exhausted, and Kai stared at me.

"All right, I'll ask my uncle if he can arrange something," he told me.

"Really? You'll help?" I asked.

"Only because you saved the bird," he said. "Even if it was a stupid thing to do, and makes you an idiot."

I grinned. Kai was being nice to me. It was amazing. We were practically friends now.

CHAPTER

FOURTEEN

A boat landed at our beach, and I waved at Doug, who was at the helm. It was big, much larger than the fishing boats that usually bobbed about on the harbour. On its side were the words *Inter-Island Vehicle Recovery Boat*. According to Kai, it usually collected broken cars from the surrounding islands and took them to the mainland to be fixed. Luckily for us, it was a quiet week.

Doug rolled the ice-cream van down a ramp. The sea was choppy, and it had been too difficult for him to negotiate his way around the rocks at the north side of our island. We'd have to think of some other way to get the van there. Hopefully Mum would stay asleep long enough for us to make it to the other beach.

The ice-cream van settled on the sand, and Doug sped back to the mainland. I hopped into the cab and looked around. There was a stick that worked the indicators, a dial to turn on the headlights, and a big, red unlabelled switch. I hovered my finger over it. The temptation to press it was irresistible.

A loud jingle boomed out of a speaker on the roof.

"Turn it off!" shouted Margot.

I pressed the switch again, and silence returned to the beach. Margot climbed in beside me and tutted. It was a good thing the ice-cream maker was off, because her glare would have melted everything.

"You've driven before, right?" I asked Margot, to distract her from wanting to kill me.

"Yes, although not a van exactly... It was more of a ride-on lawnmower, but it's pretty much the same thing. I'll do the pedals, but you can help steer if you want."

"Don't we need a driving licence?" asked Fabien.

"Not on our own island," replied Margot. "Besides, there's nothing for us to hit here, other than sand and grass."

I turned the key and the ice-cream van vibrated into life. Margot scooched closer to me and pulled on the gearstick. The van made a horrible grinding sound. Margot thumped her foot on to one of the pedals, and I held my breath. The van jolted forwards, and I gripped the steering wheel with white knuckles. The engine groaned, and we bumped across the beach at speed. A miniature sand dune loomed up in front of us.

"Left!" yelled Fabien.

I yanked the steering wheel left. The ice-cream van rocked and wobbled from side to side. Margot jammed her foot on the brake, and we drifted over the sand dune on two wheels. Steam poured from the engine, and the temperature gauge crept up towards the red zone. Margot shoved her foot back on the accelerator, and the van wobbled on to four wheels again.

The engine cut out. Silence filled the beach. We'd broken down.

Margot popped the bonnet, and steam whooshed up at us. We were only a few metres from the grassland now, but it felt like miles.

"What do we do?" I asked Margot.

"We wait for it to cool down," she said.

I looked at my watch. It was breakfast time, which meant Mum would be getting up at any minute. We had to get the van off the beach, and fast.

"Let's try pushing it," I said.

"But it looks heavy," worried Fabien.

Margot assessed the beach. "We might be able to nudge it down the slope, if I put it into neutral. Gravity should do most of the work."

I wasn't sure I understood what she meant, but

I ran to the back anyway, and pushed against the bumper. A fly landed on the windscreen wiper mockingly. The van didn't budge.

Margot and Fabien came over to help, and the van's wheels started to turn. Its bald tyres slipped over the grains of sand. I held my breath and pushed harder. The van inched slowly across the beach, and then started to pick up speed. I leaned back a bit as the wheels turned faster and faster. Margot let go, and the van barrelled away from us. I ran along behind it and watched it rock.

The ice-cream van bumped on to the grass, and the jingle blasted out of its speakers again. I dived through the open door as the van started to slow, and fumbled around for the switch. The bumpy ground must have knocked it on again.

As the sound died, Margot clambered inside after me, ripped a plaster off her knee and stuck it over the switch to hold it in place.

"That's gross!" said Fabien.

"That's necessary, if we don't want Mum and Dad to hear," she said.

We waited a few minutes for the engine to cool down, and then I tried the keys again. The ice-cream van turned on with a groan. I peered at the temperature gauge, and saw it was already in the orange zone. Gently, Margot pressed her foot on the accelerator, and we crept up the grassy hill in front of us, inch by inch. A minute or so passed, and the van conked out again.

"Somebody should go back to the house and make sure Mum is still asleep," I said.

"Good idea, but it'll have to be you, Luna," said Margot.

I turned to see what Fabien was doing, and found him sitting bolt upright, like a meerkat, his eyes fixed on something in the distance. I followed his gaze and saw a goat in front of us. Fabien tensed with excitement, and I sighed. There was no way he'd make it back to the house without getting distracted. Margot was right: I'd have to go myself.

"Meet you at the north beach," I said to Margot.

I'd barely taken two steps before I saw a figure heading towards us, and my tummy tightened. Even from a distance I could tell it was Mum. I tore across the grass towards her, quicker than I'd ever run before. A big pair of sunglasses covered her eyes. I hoped she hadn't spotted the van yet.

"Mum!" I yelled, colliding with her legs.

I spun her around, so she was facing the opposite direction, and hugged her waist. She smiled warily and patted my head. Behind her, Margot fanned the van's engine frantically.

"What's got into you? Where are Margot and Fabien?" asked Mum, taking off her sunglasses. Her proper glasses weren't underneath, and I almost sighed with relief. She was pretty blind without them.

"They're…" I began.

I glanced at the ice-cream van and saw Margot close the bonnet. A second later, one of Fabien's goats scrambled on to it. Margot waved her arms in a shooing motion, and Fabien climbed on to the van after it. He bounced on the bonnet from foot to foot, and then another goat jumped up beside him, as if he was doing some sort of goat-summoning ritual.

The first goat pranced across the top of the van and headbutted the plastic ice-cream cone on the top. It flew through the air, bounced off the windscreen and clonked Margot on the head. Fabien tried to get the goats off the van, but they turned their bottoms to him, tore off one of the windscreen wipers and tried to eat it.

Mum looked over her shoulder to see what I was staring at, but I leapt up and down and tugged on her arm. "Can I go snorkelling?"

She turned back to me, just as I saw the goats trotting off with the windscreen wiper.

"Snorkelling?" she asked.

"Yes, or scuba diving?" I said.

Margot and Fabien hopped back into the van, and I heard the engine start up.

"What's that noise?" asked Mum, trying to turn around again.

"It's my stomach," I said, pulling her back towards the house. "Can you make me some breakfast?"

"It's a kind of buzzing…" she said, brushing me away.

"Maybe it's a big bee," I replied.

"No, it sounds mechanical. Like a car…" said Mum.

I laughed loudly to disguise the noise of the engine. "That's silly. There aren't any cars on the island."

"But it definitely sounds like one," she said, trying to turn around yet again.

I spotted a plane high above us and pointed.

"Look! It must be that."

The van disappeared down a hill, and the sound was muffled. Mum shook her head, and then started back towards the house to make breakfast. I waited until she was out of sight, and then sneaked off to find the van. The boiling heap had made it to the edge of the north beach, where it shot out steam like an overheated whale.

Fabien offered me an armful of seaweed, and we draped it over the van as camouflage. It sizzled on the bonnet, and filled the air with salt. I stepped back to look at the van. It stuck out like a sore thumb.

"We'll have to think of something to keep the yoga guests away," I said.

"And the goats," muttered Margot.

"I really hope the windscreen wiper doesn't give them tummy ache," said Fabien.

I checked that the remaining one was still attached and, as I did, I noticed a scrap of paper pinned under it. The corner had been nibbled, but the rest was still OK. I read the message scrawled on the front. It was for me.

Luna, meet me tomorrow lunchtime at The Wig and Pen. Kai.

CHAPTER

FIFTEEN

"Is Kai here?" I asked Heidi the next day, as Mum settled down to check her emails.

"Yes, he's out the back," said Kai's mum.

I walked around to the back of The Wig and Pen, and slipped through the gate into a little yard. There was no sign of Kai, so I went to find the seagull. It squawked at me and pecked the bars of the cage, as if asking for food. I noticed it was standing on both feet, and wasn't a bit wobbly any more. It stretched out both its wings and flexed them.

A door opened, and I looked up as Kai stepped into the yard.

"He's well enough to release now," said Kai.

"Is that why you asked me here?" I replied.

Kai didn't say anything. Instead, he drew back the bolts on the cage, and opened the door. I stepped back, as the gull perched on the edge of the bars and stretched its wings again. It looked unsure, like it didn't know whether to leave or not.

"You'll be OK," I told him.

The seagull squawked and then took off into the sky. I watched it soar above the roof of The Wig and Pen, and disappear behind the chimney stack. Part of me wished we could have kept him as a pet, but I knew setting him free was the right thing to do.

"So, are you serious about opening a donkey sanctuary?" he asked me eventually.

I nodded. "Of course."

"Wouldn't it just be easier to get a dog?" he asked.

I took a deep breath, and explained to Kai how donkeys had been Granny's favourite animal, and how they reminded me of her, and how I wanted to help donkeys just like they did at the sanctuary that I'd been to back in England. My eyes got all blurry as I thought about Granny, and how much I missed her. She'd have known how to make Dad feel better. Everything had been so much better when she'd been around.

"I know where you can get a stage," said Kai.

"You do?" I replied, looking up at him.

Kai nodded, and walked over to the gate. "Follow me."

"Do we need the bikes?" I asked.

"No, it's not that far," replied Kai.

I followed Kai out of the yard and on to the high street. We passed the butcher's, the fishmonger's and the charity shop, before we reached a large building with boarded-up windows, and a padlock on the door.

Kai took a key out of his pocket and turned it in the lock. I hung back as the door creaked open and dust swirled up at us. A sign above the entrance said *Wishnook Community Theatre*.

"My dad used to own this place," explained Kai. "He ran an amateur dramatics club in the evening, and the village used to put on plays throughout the year. Nobody wanted to do it after he died. Mum can't bring herself to sell it, so the place has been empty for the last three years."

"That's so sad," I replied.

Kai nodded. "Sometimes I forget my dad's voice, but then I come in here and I remember it again."

For a moment I wasn't sure what to say. Kai's eyes glazed over, like he was lost in a memory. I wished I could make him feel better. He looked lonely all of a sudden.

Kai shook his memory away and turned to me. "What about your dad? Why does he never come to the mainland?"

"He's been really sad since Granny died, so he doesn't like talking any more. Sometimes it feels like he's disappeared, even though I can see him. I'm worried that one day I might forget him too, or at least what he used to be like," I said.

"Maybe the festival will help bring him back," said Kai.

He stepped through the door and disappeared into darkness. I took a deep breath and followed. It was so dark that Kai was already halfway across the room by the time I could see properly again. I bumped into rows of dusty chairs as I crept down the aisle towards a curtain at the far end. It hung from the ceiling and rippled in the breeze from the door. Kai yanked on a cord and pulled the curtain open.

A small stage appeared in front of me. It had metal legs, and a black wooden top that came up to my knees. I bent down and touched it. The stage seemed to fit together like the pieces of a jigsaw. It even had little wheels on the bottom.

"It's lightweight but strong, and easy to move," said Kai. "I can get Doug to bring it to the island for you."

I looked at him, mouth open. "You mean we can borrow it?"

"It's just gathering dust here," said Kai. "If

you're having a proper festival, then you need a proper stage. I don't want to fall through anything when I'm singing."

"Thank you," I told him.

He nodded, and started to unclip the pieces from each other. I bent down and helped him. The legs folded up underneath the top of the stage, like a collapsible table. It was perfect for the festival.

"You can look in the prop room too, if you want," said Kai.

The prop room was behind the stage, and was so full that I could barely open the door. There were rails of clothes, hats, masks, furniture and hand-painted scenery. A fake tree stood next to a real motorbike, which had a vase of plastic flowers on top. Behind them all was a Ferris wheel. It was the same size as me, and made of little Lego bricks. There was a switch on the side, which seemed to have rusted into the "off" position. I wiggled it about until it clunked on.

A motor whizzed and the Ferris wheel started to turn. I stood back and looked at it. The little carriages that swung back and forth were perfectly to scale. There was a teddy bear in one, and a handful of chocolates in another.

Kai poked his head inside the room, and smiled when he saw the wheel. "I'd forgotten about that."

"Did your dad make it?" I asked.

"Yeah, it was for a play he directed," explained Kai. "He always wanted to make a life-size one, but never had the time."

"It's lovely," I said. I remembered how Dad used to take us to see the Lego sculptures in Hamleys. We hardly ever had enough money to buy new toys, but we didn't care. We just loved seeing them all with Dad. I bet he'd have found the Ferris wheel really interesting, if only he'd come to the mainland one day.

"We could put it on the stage for the festival," said Kai.

"Do you think it would survive a boat ride?" I asked.

"Should do, if we move it on a calm day. I'll just take the carriages off," said Kai.

I jumped up and down. Now we had a stage and a Ferris wheel. Dad was going to be so happy!

We locked up the theatre, and made our way back to The Wig and Pen. Standing outside it was a group of confused-looking people. Seven cases were balanced at their feet.

"I don't suppose you know a Julie Butterworth, do you?" asked one of the ladies.

"Yes, that's my mum," I replied.

"Ah, wonderful!" she exclaimed. "Our booking email says to meet her at the harbour, but we couldn't find her."

I froze. The yoga guests were here, and they were early.

CHAPTER

SIXTEEN

I set a tray down on our living-room coffee table, and the yoga guests swarmed to it like moths around a light bulb. There were seven of them, all dressed in colourful, overly stretchy lycra. The oldest looked like Granny, only she had purple hair and a unicorn tattoo on her foot.

The unicorn lady sniffed the tea I'd made. "Is it camomile?"

"Camel-what?" I asked.

"I can't drink normal tea," she replied. "Messes with my energy."

Mum fiddled with her hands nervously. "Luna, please make Beatrix a cup of camomile tea."

I had no idea what camel-whatsit tea was, but Margot found a packet of it in Mum's handbag, and helped me make a fresh pot on the camping stove. It smelled of stale perfume and was the colour of cat wee. Unicorn Lady gulped it down happily.

After finishing the vile concoction, the yoga guests headed down to the main beach with Mum, while Margot, Fabien and I hid behind a tree to watch. We needed to make sure they stayed away from the north beach, so they wouldn't find the ice-cream van and ask questions. Maybe we could train Fabien's goats to herd them.

"They look silly," whispered Fabien.

I watched Mum sit down on a mat, and wrap her legs around her head. She reminded me of a pretzel. The seven guests sat down and tried to copy her, and a bald man wobbled into the lady next to him. She fell into a pile of seaweed, and flung it off, but it landed on the man's head. He screamed and shook his head wildly. The green wig slid down his face and flopped into his lap.

Mum untangled herself quickly, and lay down on the sand.

"Let's try meditating instead," she shrilled.

The guests copied her again, their shoulders tense.

"Imagine you're on a cloud, floating above the world," said Mum.

A woman with a seashell necklace sat up. "Clouds don't float above the world."

"OK. Imagine you're a seed, floating on the breeze," said Mum.

"What sort of seed? Are we talking small, like a poppy seed, or big, like a coconut?" said the woman.

"Are coconuts seeds?" asked one of the other guests.

"It doesn't matter! Just imagine you're any type of *small* seed," snapped Mum through gritted teeth. She took a deep breath and continued. "You are weightless. You are free. Everything is still and quiet."

A crab scuttled over Seashell Lady's hand and she screamed.

The next afternoon, Mum took the yoga guests for a dip in the sea. I waited as they waded out till the water was up to their knees, spluttering at the cold, and then sneaked off to the ice-cream van. Margot and Fabien were already there, with a big vat of custard between them. I dipped my finger into it and took a lick. It tasted of sugary vanilla.

"I hope this works," I said, as Margot poured the custard into the ice-cream maker and pressed the "on" switch.

The first batch came out lumpy, with big ice crystals dotted through it. Margot added more cream to the mixture, but this second batch was thin and sloppy. We poured more of the custard into the machine and tried again. The third lot looked nice, so I dipped my finger in it, but then choked. It tasted of mouldy cheese.

"This is harder than it looks," said Margot, wiping a bead of sweat from her forehead.

The fourth batch churned away, and I gave the ice-cream maker a sniff. So far this one didn't smell too poisonous.

A muffled noise came from outside the van, and I peered out of the window. Unicorn Lady waved at us from the other end of the beach. Next to her was a man with a patchy beard, who I knew was one of the other guests. Their hair was still wet from their swim.

My hands turned clammy. What if Mum was with them? How were we going to explain where the ice-cream van had come from, and why? One of us should have stayed behind to keep an eye on them. I'd been afraid something like this would happen.

"Is this an ice-cream van?" asked Unicorn Lady, when she reached us. It looked like she and the man were alone.

"No," I lied.

Beardy Man glanced up at the sign above the

window. "But it says Carmella's."

"Oh … well, yes, technically it is," I replied.

"What on earth is an ice-cream van doing in the middle of an island?" asked Unicorn Lady.

"It's a surprise for our dad," I said quickly.

Fabien nodded. "Yeah, he loves ice cream."

"You won't tell him, will you?" asked Margot.

Unicorn Lady looked pointedly at the cheesy rejected ice cream next to me. "I think we could be persuaded to keep quiet, couldn't we, Darrel?"

Beardy Man's tummy rumbled. "Yeah, I reckon so."

Before I could stop them, Unicorn Lady and Beardy Man reached through the window, grabbed the tub of cheesy ice cream and dug into it. I wrinkled my nose as they spooned the ice cream into their mouths, and their expressions changed from excited to confused.

"Tastes of feet," spat Beardy Man.

"I like it," replied Unicorn Lady, and she crammed another spoonful into her mouth.

Margot emptied the fourth batch of ice cream into a tub, and handed it to Beardy Man, who dug a spoon into it, had a taste and nodded approvingly. Apparently, we'd finally cracked it.

Now we just had to make sure the pair didn't say anything.

Unicorn Lady and Beardy Man sat down on the sand, and scoffed down their tubs of ice cream. By the last mouthful, Unicorn Lady had turned a little green. It served her right for being so greedy.

"I'm feeling a bit sick," she said.

"We'd better get you back to the house," said Margot.

We each grabbed one of Unicorn Lady's arms, and half dragged her through the woods, while Fabien helped Beardy Man along. Mum was outside the house when we got back, making lunch for the guests. She waved at us, and an eel slipped out of her hands. Unicorn Lady dived towards a rose bush and threw up in the petals.

"Oh, no, whatever's the matter?" exclaimed Mum.

"I think she swallowed some sea water earlier," I lied.

"The salt can have that effect on people," said Mum. "I once put a whole teaspoon of it in my tea by accident, and was sick all over a stranger's shoes. They banned me from the café after that."

Unicorn Lady threw up again.

"I think she ought to lie down," I said, and we helped her inside, where she couldn't say anything about the van, or throw up in front of Mum any more.

"Well, that could have gone worse," said Margot, after we had shoehorned the lady into bed, and were heading to our rooms.

"Yeah, we just have to hope neither of them say anything now," I replied.

The sooner the yoga guests went home, the better.

CHAPTER
SEVENTEEN

"Where are the yoga people?" I asked Margot the next day, slipping into her bedroom.

"Gone to the mainland with Mum," she replied.

"Oh good. That'll give us chance to figure out how to stop anyone else finding the ice-cream van," I replied, keeping my voice low so as not to wake Dad, who was napping in the next room.

I went to fetch Fabien, who was halfway through knitting a poncho, and we bundled on to the end of Margot's bed.

"OK, I've got an idea," whispered Margot. "We can put up signs warning of quicksand near the beach. That ought to make people turn back."

"All right, but where will we get the signs from?" I asked.

"We'll make them," replied Margot.

Fabien beamed. "I'll get my craft box! We can start on the decorations for the festival, and the posters and tickets too."

He skipped out of the room and returned a few seconds later with a big box. I peered inside at the brightly coloured tissue paper, scraps of fabric, pipe cleaners and mountains of wool. It was what I imagined the inside of Fabien's head looked like.

Margot made a start on the quicksand signs, while I cut tickets from a pile of paper, and made a special one for Mr Billionaire. I could ask Kai to sell the tickets to customers at The Wig and Pen. We'd just need to keep Mum from talking to anybody who'd bought one. Maybe we could sneak some goat poo into her jacket pocket to keep people away.

Fabien plonked himself in the middle of the floor, and began to fashion a pile of decorations, his tongue sticking out in concentration. Before long, the bedroom was filled with bunting, little jars of fairy lights, and pom-pom blankets. Margot bent wire coat hangers into headbands, and glued paper flowers on to them, while I threaded bracelets to sell and Fabien made key rings out of washed-up bottle tops.

I glanced out of the window and saw a fishing boat sailing towards us. It was bigger than *Lady Agatha*, and I wondered who was at the helm. Margot grabbed a pair of binoculars and peered through them.

"It's Doug and Kai," she said.

"They must be bringing the stage!" I replied.

We raced down to the main beach, and I waded

out into the water to meet the boat. The Lego Ferris wheel spun in the sea breeze, and the stage teetered behind it like a stack of Jenga pieces.

Doug moored the boat, nodded at us and then pulled his cap over his eyes for a nap.

"Delivery for Luna," said Kai as he jumped off the boat. "I've bought the stage, and the wheel and an old popcorn maker I found at the theatre. You can borrow that too if you want it."

"Of course! We can hide them all in the empty stable until it's time to set everything up," I said.

We carried the stage across the island, piece by piece, and then went back for the Ferris wheel and popcorn maker. Fabien tapped the wheel, and asked whether Kai would mind if he modified it after the festival to spin wool, while Margot praised its construction.

I gave Kai the tickets to sell, and asked him to collect the money for us. A few days ago, there was no way I'd have trusted him, but something had changed since I'd rescued the seagull. He'd helped us get the ice-cream van to the island, and now he was letting me borrow his dad's Ferris wheel. I knew that made us proper friends, the type you'd send postcards to, and let have the last biscuit in the packet.

Kai and Doug had only been gone a few minutes when *Lady Agatha* came into view. Margot, Fabien and I stayed on the beach and waited for Mum and the yoga guests to land. A few of them looked a bit green.

"Was that Doug I saw heading off?" asked Mum.

"Yeah, he brought Kai over to borrow a book," I said.

Mum shook her head. "Those two have far too much time on their hands."

"I'll make tea," said Margot, and together we ushered the guests up towards the house, where they'd be out of the way.

We were halfway through the woods when Bald Man stooped down and plucked something from the undergrowth. My heart plummeted as I saw what it was. In his hand was one of the festival tickets. It must have fallen out of my pocket.

"Oh, how lovely!" he exclaimed, reading it. "I didn't realise you held festivals here."

"What's that?" asked Mum.

"Nothing!" screeched Margot.

"Luna? Fabien? What's going on?" she asked.

"What festival?"

"It's… We're…" I stammered.

"We're doing a play!" said Fabien.

Mum raised her eyebrows. "A play?"

"Yes! We're doing a play that's set at a festival. This ticket is just a prop," he said.

"Imaginative play is very good for our emotional development," added Margot.

Mum nodded slowly. "Uh-huh… And where are you performing this play?"

"Here. Tonight. It's for the yoga guests," said Fabien.

Seashell Lady clapped her hands together. "Oh, lovely, dinner and a show!"

Great. Now we had to rehearse a fake play and make the props for it, all within the next six hours. It was a nightmare.

"No, no, no," said Fabien, as he read Margot's script. "Where's the goat pageant?"

"What goat pageant?" asked Margot, who had written a story about Amelia Earhart, the real-life, mysteriously missing aviation pioneer, who had somehow time-travelled to a modern-day music festival, where she started a band called

Blue Sky Pilots.

"There needs to be a glamorous goat pageant, like the festival in Itchbottom had one for sheep," said Fabien.

"That doesn't fit with the storyline," said Margot.

"Let him pretend to have a goat pageant. This isn't a real play," I reminded her.

Margot huffed and, after a quick rehearsal, we gathered the yoga guests in the living room for the performance. Mum called Dad downstairs, and he perched on the edge of the sofa and picked at a cushion. I cleared my throat, ears burning with embarrassment as I gazed out at our audience. Suddenly I felt a bit nervous.

"You look just like Amelia Earhart," I said to Margot, reading from her script.

"I *am* Amelia Earhart," she replied. "But who are you? Where am I?"

Fabien backed into the room and rustled two cabbage leaves together. A second later, a muddy goat trotted into the living room and started gobbling up the leaves. I jumped with surprise, and Margot groaned into a cushion. Mum screamed, Dad started and the yoga guests gasped.

"GET THAT GOAT OUT OF MY LIVING ROOM!" yelled Mum.

The goat jumped up on to the coffee table, and ate a Hobnob.

"He's part of the play," said Fabien. "He's one of the actors in the glamorous goat scene."

"I don't care if he's the reincarnated spirit of Mother Teresa!" yelled Mum. "Get him out!"

Fabien stood between her and the goat protectively. "That's not a very nice way to talk about him. Goats have feelings too, you know."

As Mum turned a very peculiar shade of purple, Seashell Lady jumped up and lunged at the goat. Fabien swiped her out of the way, and the goat leapt off the coffee table and bumped into Dad's knee. He gulped with surprise, and pulled his legs up. Mum collapsed into her chair and appeared to faint.

Unicorn Lady ran out of the room, down the hall and into the kitchen. She screamed as a pair of bats flew past her into the living room and circled our heads. Their wings fluttered inches above the yoga guests, and Margot stared at them in awe. Meanwhile, Fabien's goat pulled a packet of Polos from Bald Man's pocket and headbutted him in the shin.

I grabbed a lampshade and tried to lure the goat out into the hallway with it. "Look, goat, yummy, yummy."

The goat cocked its head at the lampshade and trotted after it. Margot flapped her arms behind the goat, and herded it in a straight line, while Fabien shook his head in disbelief.

"Well, this is a fine way to treat guests," he muttered.

I threw the lampshade on to the doorstep, and the goat bounded outside. The bats swooped past and disappeared into the evening clouds.

I looked back at the carnage in the living room. Seashell Lady sat shaking in the corner, while Beardy Man wafted a pot of potpourri under Mum's nose. Dad got off the sofa, and navigated around a pile of warm goat's poo. His lips twitched into a tiny smile.

"Well," said Margot. "That should have distracted Mum from asking questions about the festival."

CHAPTER

EIGHTEEN

"We've got a problem," said Kai, when Margot, Fabien and I sat down at a table in The Wig and Pen.

"The yoga people are finally going home. Can't we just be happy for a second?" I said, watching Mum load them into a minibus outside.

Kai waved a newspaper under my nose, and I leaned back to read the headline. I couldn't believe it.

New Family Throws Summer Festival!

I scanned the article. There was a quote from Frank about his band, and from the mechanic about the ice-cream van, and from some lady called Marjory, who said she was really looking forward to the whole thing. At the bottom of the article was the date and ticket price.

Kai was right. This was definitely a problem.

"Have you already delivered the papers?" I asked.

"Had to," replied Kai. "They're all over the village."

"We've got to stop Mum from seeing it," I said.

Fabien shuffled in his seat uncomfortably. "Maybe we should just tell her."

"Are you mad?" I asked.

"But she's going to find out eventually," he said.

Margot shook her head. "No, Luna's right. If we tell her now, she could still make us cancel. It's best to wait."

I spied the last yoga guest climb into the minibus. Any second now they'd be gone, and we could coax Mum safely back on to the boat and to our island. Then we just had to keep her there until the festival. Thankfully there were only five days left to go.

Then I saw Doug heading across the harbour, and I screamed. Margot flung her chair back, and I hurried after her. The minibus set off, leaving Mum an open target.

"Let's go!" I said to her.

"Wait a minute, we need to do some shopping," replied Mum.

Margot intercepted Doug mid-stride, and began asking him questions about his boats. I pointed Mum towards *Lady Agatha* and started to tug her towards it. She wriggled her arms free, and batted me away as if I were a nuisance.

"Luna, what on earth has got into you?" asked Mum.

"You can't go inside the pub," I said.

"Why ever not? What have you done?" she asked.

"I've… It's…" I began.

Fabien ran over to us, laden with paper bags. He handed them to Mum, who pulled out a cooked breakfast in a tin, and studied it in silence. I stood on tiptoes and peered inside the bags. They were filled with groceries: ham, spaghetti, toilet roll, candles. It was like he'd dashed around The Wig and Pen, and grabbed armfuls of the first things he'd seen.

"Surprise!" he said. "I've done the shopping for you."

"How have you paid for all this?" asked Mum.

"Kai said he'll invoice us later," said Fabien. "I wanted to help."

Mum smiled weakly, and lugged the groceries back to *Lady Agatha* to sort through them. I ran back and forth between the boat and The Wig and Pen, swapping all the rejected groceries for things actually on Mum's list. Eventually she ticked off the last item, and I collapsed with exhaustion.

Mum climbed off the boat.

"What are you doing?" I shrilled.

"I need to get some nails from the DIY store," she said.

"We'll get them for you," replied Margot.

Mum shook her head quickly. "No, it's fine, you've all been helpful enough."

I groaned. Mum was harder to herd than one of Fabien's goats.

Unable to stop her, Margot and I ran on ahead of Mum, and Fabien defended us from behind. We were halfway up the high street when Mum stopped on a bench to tie her shoelace. At the other end lay a copy of the *Wishnook Gazette*.

"Grab that newspaper for the fire," she said.

"Oh, you don't want that! It'll burn way too quickly," I said.

"It's good kindling," she replied.

Mum reached over for the paper, but I lunged at her and knocked it out of her hand. The bench wobbled and tipped back on its spindly legs. I braced myself, and Mum's arms spun like a windmill as we rocked backwards.

The bench crashed into a flowerbed, and I landed on Mum's head. Yellow petals filled my mouth, and I coughed up a woodlouse. Across the street, Daisy popped her head out of the newspaper's HQ. Margot rugby-tackled her back inside. I wasn't sure if Mum had seen or not.

"WHAT ON EARTH ARE YOU DOING?" yelled Mum, after checking we were both still alive.

"Luna ate a whole bag of sugar inside The Wig and Pen," said Fabien.

Mum shook her head. "Right, that's it, everyone back to the boat! Where's Margot?"

Margot reappeared from the newspaper's HQ, her hair ruffled. I wondered what she'd done with Daisy.

"I told her the street's full of wasps," Margot whispered to me, as we headed back towards the harbour. "She's gone to get her camera and boiler suit."

We were almost back at the boat when I saw somebody coming at us from the corner of my eye. I turned, ready to spin them a story about how Mum had some contagious disease and shouldn't be approached, when I realised it was Kai.

"You'd better get going soon," he panted. "I've just heard there's a storm coming."

"Are you sure? There aren't any clouds," I said.

"The weather can turn quickly," he replied.

Mum looked worried. "We'd best get a move on then," she said.

I hopped into *Lady Agatha*, relieved we were finally leaving the mainland. Across the harbour, I could see Kai's mum laying sandbags against the side of The Wig and Pen. To our left, Doug secured his boats with extra rope.

The waves rippled gently, and the sea was calm and clear.

I didn't know what everyone was so worried about.

Dark clouds rolled towards us. I watched them from my bedroom window. They swallowed the blue sky and all the sunshine. A leaf zipped past and the birds took cover in the trees. I shut my window and wrapped my cardigan around me. Kai had been right after all.

"Did we close the stable door?" I asked.

"I think so," said Fabien.

Margot paced across my rug. "What if we didn't? My aeroplane parts could get ruined."

"Maybe we should check?" I said. "Fabien, stay here and distract Mum."

He shook his head. "I want to come with you

and check my goat shelter. I made it out of some old bin bags and a fishing rod."

The sky turned steely grey. "All right. Let's try and get there and back before the storm hits."

We sneaked out through the back door and ran across the clearing into the woods. Fabien's goat shelter swayed in the wind. It was completely uninhabited. He crouched down and searched for tracks. There wasn't a goat in sight.

"Where are they?" he asked.

"They've probably taken shelter somewhere else," I replied. "Come on, we've got to get to the stables."

Rain burst from the dark sky in a torrent. I grabbed Fabien's and Margot's hands, and we slipped across the muddy ground. Wind bit our faces. The unexpected chill caught my breath.

Ping.

Something ricocheted off my shoe.

"Is it snowing?" asked Fabien.

Ping.

Ping, ping, ping.

Hailstones poured from the sky. They struck my hands, face and neck like bullets. I winced from their sting. We were under attack.

The hailstones bounced off us and the trees, and piled up on the floor. Within seconds, everything turned a hard, sparkling white. The drumming was deafening.

"Quick, in here!" I said, throwing open the door to the first stable, which had been closed all along.

We took shelter beside the stage, and peered through a small hole in the wall. The hailstones had turned to heavy rain again. I listened to the sea crash against the rocks, and hoped the ice-cream van was OK. The waves sounded so close.

Crack!

A jagged lightning bolt fizzed through the sky and turned it purple. Fabien jumped and grabbed my hand. I squeezed his hand back, shaking.

"One, two, three, four..." counted Margot.

Rumble.

"Four," I said. "Is that how many miles away the lightning is?"

"I think so," replied Margot.

"Is it coming this way?" asked Fabien.

"Probably, but it's nothing to worry about," she said, although she looked terrified.

The rain was almost horizontal now. Leaves

flew across the sky and the stable walls shook. Through the hole, I saw the trees bend almost in half. Their branches creaked menacingly. It was as if the storm wanted to break everything.

Crack!

A bolt of lightning tore through the clouds again. It split into a fork, and ripped the sky in two. I could actually hear the air sizzle.

"One, two, three…" counted Margot.

Rumble.

"Three miles," I said.

Crack! Rumble.

Rain thudded against the roof.

Crack! Rumble.

"I really don't like this," said Fabien. "We shouldn't have left the house."

The storm was right on top of us now.

Crack! Rumble.

Bang!

I screamed as lightning struck the tree next to us with the loudest noise I'd ever heard. It lit the trunk a fiery orange, and split it in half. Shards of wood flew through the air, the size of javelins. Branches fell like confetti. I braced myself as half of the tree fell towards us.

The tree crashed straight through the stable's roof and flattened the Lego Ferris wheel. I dived across Fabien to protect him. A huge branch crushed my foot, and pinned me to the ground. Pain pulsed through me, and I let out a cry.

"Luna! Are you OK?" yelled Fabien.

I tried to pull my foot free, but the pain got worse.

"Help me!" I yelled.

Margot rushed over to me. There was a gash above her eyebrow, and a huge splinter in her shoulder. She lifted the branch off me with a wince, and I tugged my foot free. Blood soaked the hem of my jeans. I took a deep breath and wriggled my ankle. The pain made me cry.

The roof creaked ominously above us. I closed my eyes and wished we were back in London, at our old flat, with our old boring lives. Suddenly, coming to the island felt like one big mistake.

Margot held a section of the stage above our heads, and we huddled beneath its armour. Eventually the thunder quietened, and the rain turned to drizzle. I rolled up the leg of my jeans with shaking hands, and inspected my ankle. It was red and swollen, with a big graze at the top.

I couldn't see any broken bones.

"I think it's just sprained and badly bruised," said Margot.

"Are you OK?" I asked.

She pulled the splinter out of her shoulder, and bit down on her lip. "Yes," she croaked. "Yes, I think so."

"What about the stage?" I asked.

Fabien inspected the piece we'd been sheltering under. There was a crack through the centre of it. I staggered to my feet and looked around. Lego bricks carpeted the floor, and my stable lay in tatters. Everything was ruined.

CHAPTER

NINETEEN

I leaned back against my pillow, and the doctor inspected my ankle. He'd come all the way from the mainland to check me over, but I still felt terrible. It would take ages to repair my stable. Worse than that, I'd have to tell Kai that his dad's Ferris wheel was broken. Maybe the storm had been a sign that the donkey sanctuary and festival were bad ideas. Maybe I'd been fooling myself thinking they'd work.

"You're very lucky. It could have been a lot worse," said the doctor.

I didn't feel lucky. In fact, I felt wretched. Kai's dad must have spent ages building that wheel, and now it was in pieces. Kai had only just stopped hating me, but now he was going to start all over again.

"So you think Luna's ankle is OK?" asked Mum, who was huddled at the top of my bed with Margot and Fabien. Dad stood in the doorway, even paler than usual.

"It just looks bruised," said the doctor. "Keep applying ice and it should be fine in time for your festival."

"What festival?" asked Mum.

I groaned and pulled the duvet over my head.

Things couldn't get any worse.

"The festival you're holding here next week," said the doctor. "I hope Kai's been passing the money on to you."

"What money?" asked Mum, and she whipped the duvet off my head. "What's going on, Luna?"

The doctor rummaged in his briefcase and pulled out one of the tickets we'd made. He handed it to Mum, and her face turned red with embarrassment. "Didn't you know about this?" he asked.

I watched Mum's expression turn angry. "Please tell me you children haven't been charging people for a pretend festival."

"It's not pretend!" exclaimed Fabien. "It's a real festival. I've made bunting and everything. We even had a Ferris wheel, until the storm destroyed it."

"A Ferris wheel…" croaked Dad.

"It was made out of Lego, but it really spun," said Fabien.

"Don't be ridiculous!" said Mum. "You can't charge people ten pounds to come and see a heap of Lego."

"But there's bunting!" said Fabien.

"We thought the festival might make Dad feel better," I said, deciding to leave out the part about my donkey sanctuary.

"Is this festival the reason you ran off in the storm?" asked Mum.

"We wanted to check the stage was OK," I said.

Mum turned to Dad. "Do you see what you've done? Your daughter nearly broke her leg because of you."

"It's not Dad's fault," said Margot.

I sat up and leaned towards the doctor as everyone argued. "Can you make sad people feel better, or are you the wrong sort of doctor for that?"

"Who's sad?" asked the doctor.

Dad cleared his throat above the racket. "I am."

Everyone stopped talking and stared at him. It was the first time Dad had said it, at least aloud. I wanted to leap out of bed and hug him, but my ankle throbbed too hard.

Dad and the doctor went out into the hallway. Mum stared after them for a moment, and then busied herself by fluffing my pillow. I held my breath and wondered what she was thinking. She still seemed angry.

"From now on, there's to be no more nonsense about festivals," she said.

"But, Mum—" I began.

"But nothing," she said. "It's nice that you were trying to help your dad, but the people who bought your tickets are expecting a real festival."

"It *is* a real festival," I said.

Mum shook her head. "I know you think it is, but you're only ten. You can't organise a proper festival."

"But—" started Margot.

Mum raised her hand. "I don't want to hear any more about it. And you're all grounded for running out in the storm."

I put my head back under my duvet. The festival was over, and with it my dream of opening a donkey sanctuary.

CHAPTER

TWENTY

We were grounded. I stood at my window and stared out at the beach miserably. It was the day after the storm, and the island looked more battered and bruised than my ankle. I closed my eyes and thought about the festival. It was just a dream now.

My bedroom door swung open, and Margot flopped down on my bed dramatically. There were dark bags underneath her eyes. She buried her face in my pillow and huffed.

"We're prisoners!" she mumbled.

Fabien sneaked in too, and perched beside Margot. "My goats must be starving. They're used to me putting out food for them now."

I patted him on the shoulder. "I'm sure they'll be happy eating all the fallen branches."

"How long do you think they'll keep us in here?" he asked.

Margot lifted her head from my pillow. "I don't know, but Mum's pretty mad at us for running off and for keeping the festival a secret. It could be years."

Voices floated up through my bedroom window, and I looked outside again. A dozen or so people were marching towards the house, armed with brooms, and mops, and rubbish bags. I squinted and saw Kai at the front, followed by his mum, Doug, Daisy Gifford, the charity shop lady and some of the fishermen. For a second I wondered if they were a mirage.

Kai waved at me through the window. "All right, Luna?"

"What are you doing here?" I called to him.

"Doc Ted said the island had been hit badly by the storm, and you'd got hurt," said Kai. "We've come to help fix everything and check you're OK."

"All of you?" I asked.

"That's what friends are for," said Daisy. "Plus, this will make an excellent cover story for next week's paper."

I couldn't believe that all these people had come to help. They barely knew us. We were just the weird family who lived on the island. Seeing them made me feel all warm inside.

"Come down," yelled Kai.

"We're not allowed to leave our bedrooms," I told him. "Mum's grounded us."

I heard the front door open, and Mum appeared on the doorstep. She wobbled with shock at the sight of everyone. Dad poked his head out of the window next to ours and looked just as surprised. His eyes sparkled as the mainlanders explained that they'd come to help.

"Don't just sit there, kids. Come down and help everyone," Mum yelled.

I hobbled down the stairs and staggered out into the sunlight. It had only been twenty-four hours, but being outside had never felt so good. Mum fetched me a chair from the living room, and I sat sorting through the bags of rubbish she'd collected earlier from the beach, making piles of anything that could be recycled.

Edna, one of the ladies who'd organised the Cakeathon, shimmied up a ladder behind me and began reattaching one of our drainpipes. I watched her in awe, and then ducked as Farmer McAndrew hosed off the wall behind me, almost soaking me in the process. I was only half convinced it was an accident.

"I told you the storm was going to be bad," said Kai.

"Yeah, about that," I said, and then broke the news to him about the stage and Ferris wheel.

"Oh," he replied, quietly.

"I'm so sorry. I never would have put them in the stable if I'd known the roof was going to cave in," I said.

"It's not your fault," replied Kai. "The chances of lightning hitting that tree must have been a million to one."

"But they were your dad's," I replied.

I knew how upset I'd be if something had happened to one of the ornaments that Granny had left me.

"I can rebuild the Ferris wheel, and the stage can probably be fixed," he said. "We've still got a week before the festival."

"No, we haven't," I replied. "It's off."

"What do you mean?" asked Kai.

"Mum found out and she's forbidden us from doing it. She thought it was a joke. Anyway, there's no point now. It'll take more money than we can raise to fix the stables. I'll never get to open my donkey sanctuary."

"So you're just giving up?" asked Kai.

I sighed. "It's all too much hassle."

"Well, maybe we shouldn't be friends after all, if you're just going to quit," he said and, with that, he marched away.

CHAPTER

TWENTY-ONE

Kai's words rang in my ears when I woke up the following morning.

I crept out of bed and hobbled across the corridor to Margot's room. She was still asleep, buried under her duvet like a hedgehog in hibernation. I poked her through the quilt, and she groaned.

"It's six o'clock, Luna," she muttered, checking the time.

"I've got a plan to save the festival," I said.

She poked her head a little further out of the covers. "Will you still have it in an hour?"

"We have to show Mum that the festival is real," I replied. "We'll patch up the stage, and decorate the beach, and show her how serious we are."

"All right, but do we have to do it now?" asked Margot.

"Yes, we've got to do it before she wakes up. Otherwise who knows when we'll get the chance to escape?" I said.

"All right, all right," she mumbled.

Fabien was much easier to convince. He sprang out of bed at lightning speed and piled the decorations into our arms. There was even more bunting than before, and a few knitted cushions for people to sit on. I could barely hold them all as we made our way down to the north beach, over fallen branches and scattered flowers.

Margot and I carried the stage into place, piece by piece, and began to patch it.

"Lucky I've got my woodwork badge from Guides," said Margot as she carefully nailed a section of the stage into place.

"Really?" I replied.

"I thought you knew. Don't you remember the model plane I built out of plywood?" she asked.

"Oh, I thought it was a bus," I said.

Margot waved her hammer at me. "A bus?"

I left her with the stage, and went to help Fabien with the decorations. We twisted fairy lights up beanpoles, dug them into the sand and strung bunting between them. Triangles of red, white, green, blue and yellow wool fluttered in the wind, next to the twinkling lights.

The stage wasn't as badly damaged as I'd thought, and with a few nails it looked as good as new. We pieced it together on a flat bit of sand, out of the tide's reach, and stood back to admire our work.

The beach twinkled magically. It really did look

ready for a festival.

"Should I go and get Mum?" asked Fabien.

"Yes, I think it's time," I replied.

Mum surveyed the beach. "You did all this yourselves?"

"Yes, together," replied Margot.

"It looks very pretty," she said.

"So does that mean we can have the festival?" I asked, hopeful.

Mum twitched her lips side to side in thought. "Who are you going to get to play at this festival? Have you thought about food? Drinks? Who's going to clean up afterwards?"

"We've got musicians, and we're going to make ice cream, and hot dogs," I said.

"If we can figure out how to keep them from exploding in the microwave," added Margot.

"And we'll clean up afterwards," said Fabien. "Promise."

Mum prodded the stage, and seemed impressed that it didn't topple over. "I don't know whether to be cross that you've done this all in secret, or impressed by your creativity."

"Impressed," said Margot.

I nodded. "Yes, definitely impressed."

"OK," said Mum. "You can have the festival. But you're not to argue if anybody asks for their money back."

Fabien, Margot and I leapt into the air and screamed.

I was going to get my donkey sanctuary after all!

CHAPTER
TWENTY-TWO

Kai dragged a hay bale across the north beach, and positioned it in front of the stage for seating. It was the morning of the festival, and we were busy setting things up. Thankfully my ankle was almost back to normal now, and just in the nick of time.

"Present from Farmer McAndrew," he said. "There're a few dozen more in the boat."

"Really? Why would he give us those?" I asked.

"I told him The Rocking Pensioners are playing," explained Kai. "He's their biggest fan, so he donated the hay."

"I thought Mike the mechanic was their biggest fan," I said.

Kai shrugged. "Everyone loves them. I've brought the money from your ticket sales, by the way."

He handed me a biscuit tin and I opened the lid. A pile of notes burst out of the top, and I stuffed them back in quickly. It was the most money I'd ever seen in my life! There had to be hundreds and hundreds of pounds inside.

"Have you counted it?" I asked.

"No, but it looks like a lot," he said.

I handed Margot the money to deal with, and

she nearly fell over in shock. "This'll definitely help with the plane," she said.

"And my sanctuary," I told her.

Margot waved her hand at me. "Yes, yes, that too."

I left her to stare at the cash, and went to fetch the other bales from the boat. It was barely light, but we still had so much to do. There was bread to butter for the hot dogs (Margot said we could save nine pence per customer if we didn't use proper rolls), custard to make for the ice cream, and signs to put up so people wouldn't get lost. Then one of us had to wait for the bands and guests to arrive. I'd found a money belt in Mum's wardrobe, so we could sell extra tickets if someone hadn't bought one.

Fabien bounced past us, and marked out the arena for his own glamorous animals contest. It had taken me and Margot ages to convince him not to enter it himself. I wasn't sure I could take the embarrassment of him declaring himself the winner.

"I'll go and wait for the bands and guests," I said, after wolfing down a bowl of cornflakes.

Brice and his brothers were the first to arrive.

I led them towards the festival area, and Margot swooned as they lumbered about the stage, practising. She was clearly in love.

By mid-morning, The Rocking Pensioners still hadn't arrived. My fingers tapped nervously. It felt like I'd swallowed a big pebble. The festival was due to open in an hour, and our star act wasn't here yet.

A boat appeared in the distance, and I breathed a sigh of relief. That had to be them now. Talk about cutting it close.

Doug, who was running a taxi service for the day, moored his boat, and Daisy Gifford climbed out. The pebble in my tummy came back again. It wasn't Frank's band, after all.

Daisy flashed her camera in my face. "Another excellent cover story for the *Wishnook Gazette*," she said, handing over her ticket. "I can't wait to see The Rocking Pensioners. I'm their biggest fan."

I stared longingly across the sea, and wished they'd hurry up. Kai pointed Daisy down the path we'd marked out, towards the festival, and I sank down on to the sand. This was a disaster. The Rocking Pensioners were the reason that we'd sold so many tickets in the first place.

Doug's boat whizzed back and forth across the sea, bringing person after person, but there was still no sign of Frank's band. I collected the tickets glumly, and sold another ten to people who hadn't bought one yet. Margot squeezed my arm with excitement.

"At this rate I'll have enough money to buy a brand-new plane!" she said.

"Not if everyone asks for their money back. We can't have a festival without the stars," I replied.

"Relax, there's no way people will want a refund when they hear Brice's voice," said Margot, her eyes going all dreamy.

"I'm going to start the sausages," I said, ignoring her.

I dragged myself over to the north beach. It was so packed, I could barely see the sand. People were sitting on the hay bales, and standing between the fairy lights, laughing as they sipped glasses of lemonade.

Fabien grabbed a microphone from the stage, and bounced over to the show arena. I groaned. He was wearing his sheep costume again, but had smartened it up with a bow tie.

"Ladies and Gentlemen, does and bucks, boars and sows, cockerels and hens," he rambled. "Please can all the glamorous animals make their way into the show pen."

I watched as Farmer McAndrew led a small, hairy pig into the enclosure. Kai's mum followed with one of his rabbits, and then the charity-shop lady with her dog, Kevin, and one of the fishermen with a live lobster.

Fabien perused the animals, and held the lobster up to get a better look at it. I winced as the lobster clicked its claws, and grabbed the end of Fabien's nose. The crowd gasped. That had to hurt.

"Owwww!" he cried. "Owwww! It's got my dose."

Fabien leapt across the enclosure with the lobster still attached to him. The fisherman ran after the pair, and tried to pull the lobster off. I watched as it tightened its grip. Fabien howled again.

"Let go, Stanley," said the fisherman.

I glanced at Daisy, who was next to me, taking photos of the show. "Stanley?"

"It's the only lobster Jim's never been able to

sell. Says it looks like his old uncle, so he keeps it in a special tank and feeds it clams," she said.

"Oh, OK," I replied.

The fisherman finally managed to drag Stanley off, and the end of Fabien's nose throbbed an angry red colour. He clutched it with his fingers, eyes watering, and glared at Stanley. The crowd burst into laughter and applauded, as if they thought it had been a stunt.

"He's disqualified for trying to kill the judge," muttered Fabien, turning his back on the lobster.

Jim clasped his hand over the lobster's head, protectively.

Fabien assessed the other animals, declared Farmer McAndrew's pig the winner and then stuck his face in a bucket of ice.

I checked Fabien's nose was still properly attached, and then went to cook the sausages. There was still no sign of The Rocking Pensioners, but at least the barbecue would distract everyone for a bit. The sausages hissed and sizzled away until they turned black at the edges. I flicked one into a slice of bread, and folded the bread in half.

"Have you got anything for vegetarians?" asked somebody.

"Of course!" I replied. "We've got lettuce, tomatoes, cucumber…"

"Anything other than plain salad?" she asked.

Daisy came over and inspected one of the hot dogs. "Don't you have any proper buns? This is just a burnt sausage in some bread."

"But it tastes delicious!" I said.

I bit into one, and the sausage scalded my lip. I jumped up and down, waving my hand in front of my mouth. When the feeling returned to my tongue, I gagged. The sausage tasted burnt, and the bread soggy.

"I didn't pay ten pounds just to watch your brother get his nose pinched by a lobster," said one of Daisy's friends.

A crowd started to form around us, and people prodded the bread. I tried to say something, but my mind went blank. People were starting to revolt.

Suddenly a casserole dish clattered down next to me, and I turned to find Dad standing at my shoulder. He lowered another dish on to the table, and I peered inside. Whatever it was smelled of warm spices.

"Anyone for Dad's home-made chilli?" called

Mum from beside him. "We've got a vegetarian one too."

I gaped at them. Dad had cooked the chilli! I wondered what had got into him.

"I'm sorry I've not been a very good dad lately," he told me. "It might take some time, but I'm going to try and be better from now on."

I wrapped my arms around his waist. "I've missed you."

"Me too," he replied.

He and Mum took over the food stand, and I went to help Kai in the ice-cream van, full of happiness. A queue of people formed outside the window, their purses open. I shoved a cone under the ice-cream maker, and pressed the button. The ice cream poured through the nozzle, and landed in a wonky blob inside the cone. At least it didn't smell of Stilton.

"Give the cone a wiggle," said Kai.

I grabbed a new cone, and tried again. This time the ice cream formed a swirly tower, but then the peak slid sideways and fell on to my shoe. It took a good seven goes to get it right, but eventually my ice creams started to look like Kai's.

Brice and Brothers took to the stage and the

queue disappeared to watch them. I closed the van for a bit and headed into the crowd to make sure everything was OK. Maybe I could keep them and Kai playing all afternoon, so people wouldn't notice that The Rocking Pensioners were missing? It was the only idea I had.

Margot danced over to me, a ring of flowers in her hair. She'd put on some make-up, and her lips were a rosy red. I followed her gaze towards Brice.

"Aren't they brilliant?" she shouted, over the crowd.

"Yeah, great," I said. "But I can't believe Frank's band hasn't turned up."

"Oh, they're here," she said, still not really looking at me.

My heart leapt. "They are? Where?"

Margot shrugged. "Dunno. I pointed them in the direction of the north beach, but I ran on ahead. I needed to get here to see Brice. I mean, to see Brice's band."

I clenched my fist and resisted the urge to thump her. Our star act was here after all, but Margot had lost them.

"Margot, you stay here and keep an eye on

everything. Fabien and I will look for the band," I said.

"All right," she replied, although I wasn't one hundred per cent sure she was actually listening.

I hurried through the crowd to fetch Fabien. Kai was due to go on any minute now, and straight after that it would be The Rocking Pensioners' turn. There wasn't much time to get them ready.

We raced back to the main beach, and looked for signs of the ageing band. A trail of footsteps curved across the sand, and disappeared in the direction of the house. There was an indent next to them, like it had been made by a walking stick. We followed the tracks up towards the house, and I saw the front door was slightly ajar. A clattering noise came from inside.

"No, I need a bigger spoon," said a voice.

I poked my head inside the kitchen, empty of bats now, and found The Rocking Pensioners raiding the cupboards. They turned to look at me, and Frank bumped his head on the extractor fan in surprise.

"What are you doing?" I asked them.

Frank wobbled into the hallway, clutching his head, and Gwen followed him out with an armful of spoons, pots, and a cheese grater.

"We left Joe's washboard at home, so we need to find a new instrument for him," explained Gwen.

"I'm quite good at playing the spoons, but Frank says they're too quiet," said Joe.

"That's why he's going to play the pots too," said Gwen. "Your sister said it was OK for us to have a poke around, and take what we needed."

I shook my head with exasperation. Margot had probably been so busy thinking about Brice that she'd not actually listened to them.

"Are you going to play the cheese grater as well?" asked Fabien.

Joe snorted with laughter. "Don't be silly! That's for my cheese," he replied, and he pulled out a slab of Red Leicester from his pocket.

I hurried them all along the hallway. "You're supposed to be on stage any minute."

"Cripes, best get down there!" said Frank, and he hobbled outside as quickly as his false hip would allow him.

We made it back to the beach and I collapsed next to Margot on one of the hay bales. Kai was halfway through a song, and was even better than

I'd remembered. The crowd were clapping along. I caught my breath and joined in.

A few songs later, Kai took a bow and The Rocking Pensioners doddered on to the stage. The crowd roared with delight as Frank started to strum on his guitar, while Gwen blew into her flute, and Joe clicked a pair of ladles together. It took me a while to work out that they were playing Lady Gaga's "Poker Face".

"Let's see everyone on their feet," shouted Gwen, dropping her flute for a moment.

Brice pushed his way through the dancing crowd, and stretched his hand out to Margot. "Wanna dance?" he asked.

Margot gawped at him, and looked like she might die of surprise. Brice shuffled his feet awkwardly. The sound of Joe's ladles seemed to get louder.

I elbowed Margot in the ribs, and she leapt up. "Yes!" she yelled, and then croaked, "Um ... yes, that would be nice."

"Cool," replied Brice.

He took her hand and led her through the crowd. Margot's knees wobbled into his. I stood at the back and watched everyone jig about.

They really were having fun. I grabbed Fabien and jumped to the beat with him. Mum and Dad nodded along from their hay bale.

Eventually the band stopped playing, and the crowd mobbed Frank as he left the stage. I looked around for Margot and saw her standing at the side, her face like thunder.

"What's wrong?" I asked.

"That boy is an absolute moron," she said. "He thinks a Porsche 918 Spyder is the best mode of transportation ever made. That's a *car*. He didn't even know what Concorde was."

I laughed. "I think that might be the shortest romance ever."

Suddenly I heard a buzzing noise overhead, and looked up. A small plane dipped its wings and circled the island. I turned to Margot. This had to be something to do with her.

Margot clasped her hands together. "It's a plane!"

"What's going on? Who is it?" I asked.

The plane descended towards the main beach, lights flashing. Surely it wasn't going to try and land? I watched as it got lower and lower.

It was coming down.

CHAPTER

TWENTY-THREE

I followed Margot down to the beach. The plane was really low now. It banked left and flew back out over the sea.

"It's a Caravan!" she exclaimed.

Fabien squinted at the plane. "It looks more like a plane to me."

Margot shushed him. "The model is a Cessna 208 Caravan."

The red plane drifted down through the sky. Its propeller whirled, and the lights on its wings flashed red. It wobbled to the left, and then to the right. Any second now it was going to touch down.

I clutched Margot's arm in fear. "It's going to crash!"

"Don't be silly," replied Margot. "They can land on water."

As she said this, I noticed that the plane had a pair of floats at the bottom. They looked like huge metal bananas. I held my breath as they skimmed the water, and braced myself for a huge splash. Instead, the plane glided across the surface like a swan, leaving nothing but a neat line of froth behind it.

Its propeller slowed, and the plane bobbed

towards us. Margot clutched my hand and grinned wildly. I thought she was going to burst with excitement.

The plane pulled on to the shore, and its pilot climbed out.

"Good afternoon!" bellowed the man. He was old, and wearing a pair of knitted slippers. I peered at them. They were in the shape of dolphins.

"Mr Billionaire!" yelled Fabien.

"You came," I said.

"Of course. I couldn't miss the event of the year," he said.

Margot rushed over to the plane, and marvelled at its propeller. She was beaming. This was like all her Christmases rolled into one.

"That was brilliant!" she exclaimed.

Mr Billionaire smiled. "Why, thank you."

"Can I sit in the plane?" asked Margot. "Just for a second?"

"We can take it for a spin, if you want," said Mr Billionaire.

Margot's entire body tensed with excitement. The veins in her neck bulged, and she turned a hot, bright red. I was pretty sure she'd stopped breathing. It was a wonder she didn't explode then and there.

"Areyoukiddingofcourseldo," she said.

"Sorry?" he said.

"Yes!" she screamed. "Yes, yes, of course I do!"

"Splendid," replied Mr Billionaire. "Best check with your parents first, though."

I bit my lip. Margot might have loved planes, but that didn't mean *I* did. I wasn't even sure how they stayed up in the sky. It always seemed like some sort of magic trick. I wondered whether Mr Billionaire was a good driver.

Margot hurried back to the festival, and returned a few minutes later with Mum. She seemed a bit giddy from the adult punch Kai's mum had brought, and didn't take nearly as much convincing as I'd thought she would to agree to our flight.

"Just above the island," she said. "And no stunts, Margot."

"This is the best day of my life!" my sister squealed, clearly recovered from her heartbreak over Brice.

I climbed inside and looked around. In the back, there were two rows of single leather seats, which were scuffed and had holes in them. I sat in the front row, and Fabien sat across the aisle. The cockpit didn't have a door like big planes do. I could stare straight out of the front windscreen.

Mr Billionaire got the plane ready for take-off, and Margot sat in the co-pilot seat and buried her face in a fat paper manual. Her hand hovered above the various instruments as she read it. Every once in a while, she said things like, "Oh, *there's* the fuel gauge."

I tightened my seatbelt and held on to the seat. Margot took notes as Mr Billionaire pressed buttons, turned dials and switched switches. The aeroplane's engine buzzed into life, and the dashboard flashed like the London Eye at night.

We started to move and I pressed my face to the window. It was like being on a bus, only without the screaming babies and folded-up bicycles. I wondered how fast it could go.

"Hold on tight," said Mr Billionaire.

He drove the plane straight into the sea, and we bobbed over the waves. I watched the propeller start to twirl. It went round and round, faster and faster, until the blades were a blur.

Fabien reached across the aisle and grabbed my hand. The plane tilted skywards and I looked back to the window as the sea fell away.

We were flying.

I squeezed Fabien's hand. "This is so amazing!"

"Look how small the boats are!" he replied.

They were like tiny Lego pieces. The plane circled the island and I peered down at the north beach. From here I could see the ice-cream van, and all the fairy lights, and the stage. The Rocking Pensioners were doing an encore, and the crowd was dancing together. It looked so fun and magical. I couldn't believe Margot, Fabien and I had made all of this happen.

"Margot, would you like to take the controls?" he asked.

"Me?" she spluttered.

"If you want," he replied.

Margot shook her head. "I don't think I can."

I leaned forward. "You're not scared, are you?"

"No, of course not," she said.

"Then what's wrong? This is your dream."

Margot chewed the side of her cheek, leaned back and whispered to me, "It's just... What if I'm not any good at it?"

"Impossible," I laughed. "You're the cleverest person I know. I bet you could fly the plane with your eyes shut."

She smiled, sat up straight and nodded.

I held my breath and hoped I was right. Margot took the strange gearstick and steered the plane. She yanked it and the cabin rolled sharply on to its side. I grabbed hold of the seat in front of me and screamed.

Mr Billionaire seized the other control and righted the plane. "Whoa, whoa. A little less enthusiasm, or we'll be doing a loop-the-loop."

"Don't kill us!" shouted Fabien.

"I feel sick!" I said.

Margot took a deep breath, calmed down and helped steer the plane over the woods. I saw a glimpse of the stables beneath the leaves, and the damaged roof. It didn't look too bad from the air. Maybe we'd have enough money from the festival to fix it after all.

We flew back over the festival and started our descent. The lower we got, the more I could see. Two figures were dancing together at the edge of the festival, one in red and the other blue. I couldn't be sure, but they looked an awful lot like Mum and Dad. Maybe my birthday wishes would come true after all.

CHAPTER
TWENTY-FOUR

Six Months Later

I unbolted the stable and a donkey plodded out. He bent down and licked the snow. It covered his muzzle like icing sugar.

"Good morning, Monty," I said, stroking the donkey's neck.

Monty poked his tongue out at me.

I gave him a carrot to chew, and tied a blanket across his back. The fur on his pot belly gleamed in the cold sunshine. It was hard to believe it'd been so matted and smelly when Kai had found him three months ago, wandering one of the fields.

"You're going to have a new friend today," I told him. "Another stray. She should be arriving at any minute."

Monty nuzzled my arm, and I led him down to the beach. Snow had settled on the sand and was melting slowly. Above us, an aeroplane circled, and I waved at it. The plane's wings dipped in greeting. Margot's first proper flying lesson with Mr Billionaire seemed to be going well. He'd offered to give her lessons once a month, in exchange for private yoga lessons, and more knitted slippers.

"Luna, I made your new donkey a welcome present," said Fabien, running over with a huge bundle in his arms.

I took the knitted lump. "Wow, thanks. What is it exactly?"

"It's a jumper, so he doesn't get cold," said Fabien.

A herd of goats skipped over to us. The smallest one bent his head to lick Fabien's shoe, and then butted me in the knees. I winced, and Fabien lured it away with a clump of seaweed.

"Good boy, Aristotle," he said to the goat.

I gazed out to sea and spotted a boat on the horizon. As it got closer, I saw the outline of a donkey wobble about on deck. My heart raced with excitement. The second resident of Luna's Donkey Sanctuary was almost here.

I waded out into the shallows to greet the boat. Dad guided it into the mooring and steadied the donkey. I took an apple from my pocket, and tried to coax it down the ramp and out of the boat. The donkey swayed from side to side, looked a bit seasick and then trotted on to the sand.

"Don't be scared," I told her, grabbing her

lead. "You're home now."

Monty plodded over to the new donkey and sniffed her. She brayed a happy hello. They seemed to like each other.

"What are you going to call her?" asked Dad.

"I don't know. How about Moon, because of her silver fur?" I said.

"Monty and Moon," he replied, pondering the two donkeys. "It sounds like a detective agency."

I smiled. Maybe they could solve the mystery of where Fabien's sheep costume had gone. The outfit had mysteriously vanished from his wardrobe a few months ago, along with its smell of damp earth and goat poo. I suspected Margot might have had something to do with it.

Dad went back to the house to work on his new painting, and I led the donkeys up to the stables with Fabien. Moon immediately headed for a pile of hay, and began munching her way through it. I sighed with relief. She was going to be happy here, just like Dad was starting to be.

Margot's aeroplane passed overhead, and descended towards the sea. Fabien and I left the donkeys to eat their breakfast and headed back to the beach to meet her. She was wearing an aviator jacket and had a grin wider than Australia on her face.

"Did you see me?" she asked as she clambered out of the plane.

"Yes, you were brilliant," I said.

"Thanks," she replied. "All that flying's made me hungry."

Mr Billionaire gave me a wave, and then taxied for take-off. He was going to the mainland to talk to Kai's mum about reopening the Wishnook Community Theatre. Kai was really excited about the idea, so I'd ordered him a book about how to direct plays for his birthday. I had a funny feeling his debut might involve Margot's Amelia Earhart script.

"Let's go back for lunch," I said as the plane flew out of sight. "We can start planning next year's festival."

"I've been working on a dance routine for it with the goats," said Fabien.

"Brilliant," I laughed, and the three of us headed back across the island, towards home.